Untamed Thoughts
of
A Middle Aged Housewife

A Compilation of Erotic Short Stories
from the Imagination of A House Wife!

Fiona Warren

Publisher: Inspiring Publishers,
P.O. Box 159, Calwell, ACT Australia 2905
Email: publishaspg@gmail.com
http://www.inspiringpublishers.com

A catalogue record for this book is available from the National Library of Australia

National Library of Australia The Prepublication Data Service

Author: Fiona Warren
Title: Untamed Thoughts of A Middle Aged Housewife
Genre: Fiction

Print ISBN: 978-1-922792-91-4
eBook ISBN: 978-1-922792-92-1

For a very long time I have felt like I had a piece missing. Turns out it was you!

This book is dedicated to the piece that makes me whole.

Contents

A Little About the Author!

I was a "stay at home" Mum in Adelaide South Australia. I felt very lucky that I could stay home with my kids to watch them grow up and support them into their adult years.

My kids were in primary school at the time and as they got bigger so did the cost of living. Financially we were stuck. My kids needed new shoes and I just didn't have the money.

One of the Mums I talked with regularly at the primary school where my children attended, and I had become friends with over time offered me a job.

It was too good to be true. I could work my own hours, I could do most of my work from home and I could earn some money to help out my family. Perfect!

She was the founder of this little company, which she started years before to help keep her own family afloat. The only problem was she sold "Adult toys" through party plan.... Do you know what I mean by party plan? It's kind of like a Tupperware 'at home' party. (A bunch of plastic, silicone and rubber stuff that adult's use) 😄

I had led a very sheltered life growing up and then marrying quite young I had no experience or knowledge of these things. I was convinced I couldn't do it. She assured me I could and that she would train me herself. My husband was quite "disturbed" by the whole thing but reluctantly allowed me to try.

I threw myself into learning about the products she sold. I even made myself a party plan script (so I wouldn't look like a fool) when hosting these events.

I created a Facebook page under the name of the business..... And that was the beginning of my adventures.

My very first customer on Facebook was a young bloke. He seemed to be impressed by my knowledge and placed an order with me. Little did he know at the time I was basically a virgin in the industry.

I was so excited though. I was thrilled I had a customer.

I met with him to receive a cash payment and placed the order with my boss/friend, then delivered his order to him once it arrived.

I am very happy to report I am still in contact with this bloke and that we became very good friends and I am even God Mother to one of his 6 kids now. That was 9 years ago! (2013)

But Facebook orders weren't going to be enough. I needed to start doing parties. That's where the money was going to be.

I asked my friends to help get me started. Two of my friends jumped at the chance to host their own party for me.

I was nervous and stumbled my way through my first party, and then my second. From that moment on I was hooked. I loved it, and I was able to buy my kids the new shoes they needed with my first commission pay check.

With Each party I became more confident and soon it became 'normal' to talk about sex and all the fun stuff that goes with it. I would play hilariously funny Adult themed party games, listen to people's sex stories, answer questions to the best of my knowledge and even shared some of my own experiences at these in home events.

My parties soon became the talk of the town (or so to speak) and I was becoming recognised at my local shopping centres and almost everywhere I went someone would recognise me and say Hello. It was a good feeling to be recognised, I felt like a mediocre celebrity.

A year after joining my friend/boss informed me that her company had been nominated in the "Australian Adult Industry Awards" and that she was taking me to Melbourne (Victoria) for the awards night.

I was so excited. I paid for a haircut (I have cut my own hair for as long as I can remember to save money) I bought myself a fancy dress, new shoes, some shiny new jewellery and I must say we scrubbed up pretty well for the big night.

WE WON! Best Adult Party Plan 2014.

Seeing as I was her only working consultant at that time, I kind of took this as a personal victory too! It was so exciting. *Side note… other people joined over the years as consultants but they didn't seem to have the success that I did within the company and soon left the business.

Over the next 4 years I became busier with the party planning, which had me working almost every weekend doing parties, with the Facebook page and being a full time Mum/ wife/ house keeper/ accountant/ barber/ master chef and general peace keeper within the household. It was exhausting. But fun.

The business had won awards in consecutive years since I had started with them. I spent a lot of time interacting with people on the Facebook page and became a sounding board for quite a few people that "just needed to talk to someone". This is how I began writing short stories. I was interacting with people face to face at the parties and via messages on Facebook and I found it to be an overwhelming consistency of people wanting to be heard and even though I was a complete stranger to these people sometimes it is easier to open up to someone they didn't know and will never meet, than talk to their partners or spouse. So with all these thoughts and conversations rattling around in my mind I thought I would dabble in putting pen to paper. My first story was based on my own thoughts on what I would like "to do" If I was in that situation. I shared this to my Facebook page and received a lot of wonderful feedback, which encouraged me to write more.

I was chatting with a guy on and off over a period of a few weeks (his name fails me right now) he gave me a scenario that he would like to be involved in and asked me to come up with a story. I did!

Having worked with a few strippers while involved with the party plan business I had a basic idea of what happened and my next story just seemed to flow.

"A night with a stripper"

I shared it with my Facebook page and that also received a lot of attention. Friends and followers started giving me ideas of their own fantasies and I would write a story for them if their scenario appealed to me. *Names in my stories are changed to protect the people involved.

Over the years I have spoken to many people; so these stories may (or may not) be based on these peoples real life events. ☺

I'll let you be the judge! I think my stories have improved over the years too!

I have met some really wonderful people through my line of work and the Facebook page. One of which this book is dedicated to! I am truly grateful for the experiences I have had and the stories I've listened to and shared. Some people will never be forgotten and remain in my heart.

Sadly I am no longer working for my friend, her business paused a few years ago but is up and running again (2022) we are still really great friends too. (I was privileged to be a bridesmaid in her wedding❤) and my Facebook page is still going strong too.

I am still within the "industry" but now I manage a local Adult store!

Not as much fun as the party plan business but I feel I'm much too old to be doing that now 😄

I am still writing short stories but these days it's more about keeping my mind busy….. It's kind of like self-therapy!

Thank you for taking the time to read my little book.

I am humbled and grateful for all the support and encouragement I've had during this time, and forever in debt to those that encouraged me to write a book!

Much Love to you all. Fiona X

The Awards

1

A Little Tease

My hands would be all over you while I was kissing you. I would take your top off, kiss your neck biting a little. My hands all over your chest feeling your hard nipples then I would flick and pinch them. Then I would bite and suck them.

My hand goes lower and I can feel that you are enjoying my attention. Your cock is bulging. I rub it on the outside of your pants and you moan telling me how much you love my touch. Your arms are wrapped around me and you take my top off, exposing my bra and you look at me with those devil eyes and I kiss you hard, passionately, all the time feeling your hard cock in my hand.

I undo your pants and push them down to your knees as I push them down I follow with my kisses all the way down and kiss your belly. I look up at you and you melt a little and relax a bit more.

I kneel before you and pull your underwear down. Your long hard cock springs out and flicks my face. I smile. I place my hand around your cock and gently kiss the tip…. You moan loudly as I start to lick.

Mmmm you are my lolly pop. You grab a fist full of my hair with one hand and reach for my breast with the other and pull at my nipple. I moan. That feels so good. I am tingling all over and take all of you into my mouth. Mmmmm

My tongue slides up and down the length of your shaft. I taste you. I'm making love to your cock with my mouth and you love it.

Your grip gets tighter on my hair and you start to pull it.

I'm moaning over your cock and you seem to like that. You push my face deeper on to your cock and I look up at you. My eyes start to water "suck it harder" you say to me.

Back and forth, back and forth, up and down your cock enjoying every inch of it.

I stop suddenly and push you down on to the couch. I then start removing your pants completely. You are fully exposed to me. You are gorgeous. I stand and take the rest of my clothes off while you watch me.

I do a little show for you. Play with my breasts, pull my nipples and you show me your devil smile as you grab your shaft and pull it gently while I perform for you. I trace my hand down over my tummy to my wet dripping pussy and my fingers are cold which takes my breath away. I gasp slightly and you smile. I put my fingers in my mouth to taste my own juices.

I kneel in front of you and take you in my mouth again. I reach up and start to play with your nipples. I look up at you with my mouth full of your cock and you say "you're my dirty girl" and thrust hard into my mouth, your cock is divine and wet from my mouth. I stop sucking and place my breasts around your cock and move up and down, so your cock is sliding between my breasts. Each time it pops out the top I kiss the tip of it. I'm so wet for you. You grab my hair. I love that forceful feeling.

I can't stand it anymore. I have to have you. I stand up and mount your hard cock. It slides into my wet pussy and my juices are all over it. I grab hold of the lounge just over your shoulders to steady myself and grind my pussy harder on to your cock. It feels so good. The tip of your cock reaches that special spot inside me and I start to quiver. I grind you harder. Your breathing gets hard and fast and I can feel I'm about to release a huge orgasm. My body starts to shake and convulse as I cum. I scream out.

You grab my hips and push me down harder on your cock, you scream out "fuck yeah" as we both release. I fall into a heap on to you and gently kiss your neck. I am weak from my climax and fall to the floor.

2

Our Night With A Stripper

I don't get a chance to catch up with these two very often, so when we get together we certainly make the most of it. We decided to have dinner out and then come back to my place for a chick flick and drinks.

Kimmi and Rachel have been great friends of mine for a very long time and we have done so much together. So it's not unusual that we have a movie night. The movie we had decided to watch was Magic Mike. There is nothing better than sitting around with your girlfriends watching men dance and get their clothes off, while enjoying a few drinks.

The movie started off well, we were giggling, laughing and just having a great time. The drinks were going down nicely and we were ticking over. By the end of the movie we were all very tipsy and now because of the movie and our imaginations combined with a little naughty talk we were slightly horny too and wanted more.

I suggested we get a stripper; it was only around 11pm so there was heaps of time to enjoy a personal show of our own. The more we discussed it the better it sounded. We discussed and giggled over what requirements we wanted for our show. I remembered that I have a friend that wanted to try a stripping gig but needed some practice. The ladies wanted him, he sounded like fun and from what I've heard he has a really huge cock.

Perfect!

I phoned my friend Dan. He was keen to give it a go and was eager to come over.

While we waited for him to arrive we continued drinking and discussing in great detail all the things we wanted to do to him once he arrived, but of course would never actually have the courage to do.

About half an hour later the doorbell sounds and we all erupt in childish laughter and excitement, like school girls.

Dan came into the house and I showed him to my bedroom so he could change into his costume and get ready. He commented on the size of my king bed and said "that would hold a few at a time" and gave me a little wink. I blushed a little and thought, did he just flirt with me?

I pushed that thought out of my head and asked him if he needed anything before he started. "A drink would be nice" Dan replied

I left and shut the door to give him some privacy, and returned a few minutes later with a can of Jim Beam and Coke to calm his nerves. I knocked on the door and was given the all clear to enter the room.

It was a surprise to see him standing there, in my bedroom completely naked with his cock in his hand. He was stroking it. I quickly entered the room and shut the door behind me, I didn't know where to look, but I did manage to see he does have a huge cock. I handed him the drink and asked if I could do anything to help. I realised after I had heard my own words out loud at how inappropriate that sounded, bloody alcohol! I wasn't thinking straight.

Dan grabbed my hand and guided it to his cock. My hand opened and took hold of his enormous appendage like I knew exactly what to do. I guess my reaction was exactly what he wanted cause his hand gently came up to my face and he traced his fingers along my cheek, my breath caught in my throat as his hand went behind my head and he grabbed a fist full of my hair and pulled my face closer to his until his lips were touching mine, gently at first but then harder until I moaned a little.

He stopped kissing me and told me to get on my knees. At this point I was so damn excited and tipsy from all the alcohol consumed that I did as I was told. I knelt before him and his cock was right there, right in front of my face. My first reaction was to put it in my mouth, wow he was huge, I could barely get my mouth around it.

He grabbed the back of my head and he gently fucked my face. At that point I could hear my friends in the other room, which brought me back to reality. Wow, that could have gone a lot further if I had let it. I stood up and said to him "you'll have to finish getting ready on you own." He handed me his music and winked at me as I left the room. My heart skipped. I felt like a teenager again, and left the room a little flushed. A few minutes later I started his music, turned up the volume and we all waited for him the exit my bedroom.

The door opens and there is Dan in a cowboy costume, carrying a child's toy hobby horse. I smiled….. Did he know that I have a soft spot for cowboys?

He came into the middle of the room and starts his dance; the ladies love it and squeal with laughter and delight. Dan looks straight at me and then turned around to seductively sit on my lap, straddles his legs over mine and then drags my hands around his body and guide me to the rod of the hobby horse. The ladies squeal again. He gets off me and dances around Kimmi and starts to remove some clothing. Piece by piece his clothes are thrown to the floor.

Now Dan just has these sexy little hot pants on with the cheeks of bum exposed and his hat….….In my mind I repeat to myself several times "Please leave the hat on, please leave the hat on, please leave the hat on." He continues to dance and strut his stuff as we all giggle and laugh. He walks around the room and stops in front of Rachel, grabs her hand and places it on the front of his pants so she could feel his penis, Immediately Rachel gasps "Whoa, you're a big boy!"

Dan moves to Kimmi, then turns around and asks her to slap his ass. She does with enthusiasm and then he quickly moves to me and straddles my legs again, grabs my head and shoves it to his groin. The girls are clapping loudly and I smile at the thought that I've already been there tonight. The music changes to a new song and Dan moves to the centre of the room so his back is facing us, and then seductively pulls his pants down. I was shocked to see no G string…… He bends further and completely removes them and being cheeky looks over his shoulder to see if we are watching him. Of course we are. His pants now gone, he is completely naked. He turns to give us a full frontal view. Dan's magnificent penis is in all its glory. He certainly was a big boy!

The music comes to and end and he takes his bow. We are clapping wildly; Rachel was shouting "more, more, we want more."

Dan starts to pick up his things and I get up from my seat to help him, but the alcohol in me rushes to my head as I stand up and I lose my balance and fall to the floor, right in front of Dan. I look up at him and begin to blush; his penis was right in front of my face. Rachel screams with laughter "Go on Jess, give it to him."

Definitely the booze in me, I sit up on my knees, reach for his penis and place it in my mouth. He didn't move, only looked down at me and said "Good girl."

The ladies were in shock that I did this, but were calling out encouragement. Dan came down to my level, kneeled in front of me and kissed me with so much passion, it took my breath away. His hands were all over me. I loved this too much to stop him. He lifted my top over my head then fumbled with the clasps of my bra. He managed to undo them and then my bra fell to the floor right next to my top. My breasts were exposed and nipples erect, giving away the level of excitement.

Dan pushed me to the floor and was quick to remove my pants and underwear. I was relaxed from all the booze that was consumed earlier and then all of a sudden I feel him push my legs open and the warmth of his tongue on my clit, almost made me climax right then. I gasped with pleasure and grabbed his head to push his face deeper into my pleasure spot. I didn't care that my friends were watching me, it was exciting. Dan looked up at the other two and seductively said in his deep sexy voice "I want you two as well, clothes off ladies and join the party."

Kimmi and Rachel quickly started removing their clothing. Dan went back to eating my pussy. His tongue flicking and dancing over my clit, it was delightful. I was in heaven. Kimmi and Rachel were both naked now. Kimmi knelt beside Dan and started playing with his cock, Dan moans with pleasure into my pussy. Rachel kneels at my head; her hands reach out to my breasts and start caressing and pulling at my nipples. This was the best feeling. Rachel leans forward slightly so her pussy is almost touching my face. I take advantage of this and dive in with my tongue. Mmmmm she tastes amazing and is wet already.

Rachel leans into my face so I can really tease her pussy with my tongue. Dan looks up from pleasuring me and starts to kiss Rachel. My pussy juices that are on his face are now in Rachel's mouth. That's hot. As Dan kisses Rachel he slides his fingers inside me and reaches for Kimmi at the same time and finds her vagina and starts to finger her too. This guy is talented. Dan wants my pussy and without warning his huge penis teases the entrance of my pussy. I gasp at the size of it as he thrusts into my tight pussy. But I love the feeling of being stretched. The other two start kissing and teasing each other. I watch them as Dan fucks me harder and deeper with each thrust.

Dan pulls out and turns me over onto my knees and takes me from behind, pounding my pussy, he grabs my hair and says "take all of it you naughty girl" and slaps my ass.

Kimmi positions herself in front of me her legs spread so I can dive in and start to lick and tease her pussy with my tongue.

I put my finger in her wet cavity. As I do this Rachel sits on Kimmi's face and gasps as Kimmi starts to eat her out. We continue pleasing each other for a while until Dan says he is ready to cum.

He stands up and the three of us kneel in front of him. Dan reaches out to Kimmi and Rachel's faces and I was in between them so I start sucking him off. We sandwich him so all have our mouths on his cock.

Dan pulls our hair and moans, then he grabs his cock and starts to tug at it, taking it in turns tapping our tongues with it, he starts pulling it faster, and we were waiting there with mouths open. He started cumming, spurting all over our faces and tongues, spreading his cum all around.

Dan picked up his things and headed to the bedroom. He turned to look at us before he reached the bedroom door and said "Do you ladies want more? Are you ready for round 2? Let's try out that big bed of yours." Then he winks at me.

The fun continued in the bedroom.

Best night ever!

3

In His Room

We had been watching TV and my friend had left the room a while ago, I was curious to know what he was doing, I went to investigate.

I walked into his room and as I entered the sight before me made me stop on the spot. He was lying on the bed, naked! His eyes were closed but I didn't think he was asleep. I leaned against the doorway and just absorbed the sight before me.

He was lying on his back in the middle of the bed, one arm lying across his chest and the other was casually placed above his head. His legs were slightly parted and his manhood was quite openly on display. What a sight!

He was hard, standing at attention! I just wanted to join him on the bed but I continued leaning against the doorway, admiring the view.

He opened his eyes and saw me standing there, "Like what you see?" I blushed slightly, thinking dammit I've been busted. I smiled "I won't complain" I replied.

The hand that was on his chest moved down to his hard cock and he placed his strong hand with long fingers around his cock and started to pull gently. Watching him do this made my tummy flip and my loins started to ache. He has total control over me and he doesn't even know it. I watch as he massages his penis and I want to join in but I'm enjoying the view too much. He looks at me and pats the space next to him on the bed. I walk over to him and sit on the edge of the bed. He touches my arm and it instantly reacts with heated tingles. He has no idea what his touch does to me. My skin has electric responses from his touch.

A short burst of air is sucked into my lungs as I inhale and reach out to touch his cock. His hand moves away as mine takes its place.

He's so hard yet his skin is so soft and delicate. I start to massage his penis and I watch his face as he closes his eyes and enjoys my touch.

I was mesmerised so after a little while I have no idea how long I'd been playing with his cock I move to position myself between his legs and slowly take his cock into my mouth, sucking gently. I move my mouth up and down his cock and can feel it at the back of my throat. He likes that because both his hands grab my head and he pushes it down. I can feel his fingers tightening on my hair and this makes me moan a little. I can hear he takes a deep breath and his fingers tighten again.

I lick the length of his shaft with my tongue and kiss the tip. I love having him in my mouth. He pulls my head up by my hair and in his sexy gruff voice says "take your clothes off, I need to feel your skin next to mine."

I stood up next to the bed and started removing my clothes. He was watching every move and taking pleasure in my movements. As each item of clothing fell to the floor his eyes sparkled a little more. I stood there completely naked, he patted the spot next to him again and I quickly lay next to him. My head on his pillow we look into each other's eyes. He kisses me and I can feel my heart stop, his kiss deepens and I'm lost to him. The touch of his warm mouth to mine is the connection I have desired so greatly. I can feel his hand gently touching my skin. As he traces his finger up the side of my body it leaves a trail of electricity. He pushes me so I'm lying on my back and his finger continues to tease my skin.

Still kissing me, his fingers are exploring my stomach and then my breasts. He pinches my nipples and a breath escapes my mouth. He stops kissing me to smile and then pinches my nipple a little harder between his fingers, and watches my reaction.

His lips return to mine, his tongue flicks inside my mouth. Mmmmm my head is spinning at the enjoyment I am feeling. His hand leaves my breasts and traces a line down my stomach to my newly shaven pussy.

"Mmmmm you're smooth, so smooth" he whispers into my mouth.

I part my legs slightly to give him access to me but he doesn't take it. He runs his fingers over my vagina, teasing the lips. This feels amazing and I moan. His fingers keep tracing back and forth and every so often push a little harder.

He still hasn't parted my lips to reveal my moisture. This is driving me insane and I start to wriggle with pleasure and impatience. He lifts his head up and watches my face as I indulge in the sensation that is quite overwhelming.

His finger keeps tracing the lips of my vagina sometimes softly and then pushes hard against my clit, but still on the outside. I can feel myself becoming wetter by the second. He stops, I open my eyes to see him looking straight into them, and he smirks at me and then without warning smacks my vagina. I gasp. He quickly continues his gentle teasing. The pleasure I felt in that split second was mind blowing. He smacks my pussy a few more times and I just about explode with pleasure.

His fingers find their way into my wetness, he smiles at me "mmmmm you're so wet baby" and continues to slide his fingers between the folds of my pussy. He finds my clit and rubs it gently. I'm tingling all over as I am enveloped in the sensations this is giving me. He slides his finger down to find the opening of my pussy, teases a little then pushes his finger deep inside me. The pleasure is intoxicating. I arch my back and push my pelvis up to meet the thrust of his finger. In and out his finger slips with ease, faster and faster. My head is spinning as all the thoughts leave it, I can only concentrate on the pleasure I am feeling.

He is still watching me and kissing my neck, leaving a trail of small bites. His breathing increases slightly as I whisper in his ear "use two fingers."

He smiles as I feel him withdraw his finger and replaces it with two. Ohhh the pleasure sends jolts of tingles up my spine.

"Mmmm you love a good finger fuck don't ya baby?" he says.

"I do, but I want your cock inside me more, I want you to pound me hard" I replied

He was quick to stop what he was doing and shifted himself kneeling between my legs and before I could fully comprehend what was happening he pushed his knees right up close to my bum and guided his rock hard cock to my wetness. I could feel the tip of his cock just resting against the opening of my pussy.

I lifted my legs and he grabbed my ankles pushing my legs further apart. His knees push up closer to me and I can feel his cock about to enter me. He leans forward and pushes his pelvis toward mine and his cock fills my hole, I have instant goose bumps and exhale with a loud moan.

He also moans at the feeling of my tight pussy around his cock, he fucks me hard and the pleasure is so overwhelming. I am feeling the depth of his penis with every push it gets deeper. He pushes my legs further apart and I can feel all of him. I take the lot… all of it, right to his balls. He pounds me harder and harder, his breathing becomes faster, I can hear his pleasure increase. I place my own fingers between us and find my clit and start to massage it. The feeling of his cock pounding my wetness and the pleasure of clit play soon I can feel myself tense in preparation of cuming. My breathing and moaning get louder as does his. The continued arousing feeling that is working its way up to an explosion is almost there. My hips meet every thrust he pushes into me, my fingers move faster with experienced movements and his grip gets tighter on my ankles.

I breathe out the words "I'm coming, I'm coming," as my whole body erupts into convulsive shakes. My toes curl as every muscle in my body contracts with pure pleasure. He breathes out as I'm coming to the end on my convulsions and his body becomes rigid with his own pleasure. He moans loudly as his orgasm shakes through his body. Mine is still twitching to mirror his movements. He releases my ankles and falls to the bed next to me. He smiles at me and says "I fucking love you."

My heart almost stopped beating but then I look at him, kiss him gently on the lips and reply "I fucking love you too baby."

4

Training Night

It was a cold night at footy training and the club rooms were full of players, staff and parents waiting for their kids to finish junior training. The club rooms are heated and there is plenty of seating there for all the Mums and Dads to wait in comfort while their kids are outside getting muddy and enjoying the fun of footy.

I've been a part of the club for years, being a single Mum I like to help out where I can, working in the canteen, scoring their games and cleaning the club rooms. It keeps me busy. My kids played here when they were little, and I have watched them and their friends grow up playing footy. Some are still here as members of the adult teams, most have moved on with their lives. But I am still part of the club.

As the parents leave with their kids, the bigger players start to arrive for their training sessions. These are all A, B and C grade players, the adult players of the club that are very passionate about their game. I know them all. They all come to see me to say "Hi" before going outside to train. This is my favourite part of the night; some of these guys are absolutely gorgeous, running around in their little shorts and tight Guernseys.

We all have a great time at the club, joking around and loving life. Tonight was no different from any other night. I stood back watching them run around and kick the ball to each other. As the night progressed I do all of my tasks for the evening and gradually all the players, coaches and spectators leave. It was my job to clean the club room and change rooms before I lock up and leave. I loved this part of the night.

I turn the music up really loud and enjoy my own company while cleaning and pottering around. I cleaned all the tables and stacked all the chairs in the corner of the room so I can vacuum the carpets and then wash the floors.

While the floors are drying I head into the change rooms to clean up in there. It is always a big mess because all the players come in muddy. They shower, make a mess and leave. I don't mind though, it keeps me busy.

I grab my cleaning things and head into the change rooms. I look around to try to figure out where to start. I pick up all the wet towels and Guernsey's and put them in the clubs washing machines, and start the machines going. One machine has the towels, and the other with Guernseys. It usually takes a while for the machines to finish their cycles, but I'm in no hurry.

Not expecting anyone else to be there I was startled when I hear a noise. I call out "who's there?" No answer!

I must be imagining things.

I can still hear the muffled sounds of my music playing in the other room; the doors are locked so I know I'm safe. I go back to what I was doing when I hear another noise. I turn around to investigate and Bryan was standing there, still in his muddy footy gear.

"Oh! You scared me, I thought everyone had left. Why are you still here?"

Bryan had a cheeky grin on his face and replied "waiting for you!"

Bryan is one of the 'A' Grade players, and we playfully flirt all the time, I'm guessing he is in his mid-20's and I'm in my 40's so as I am quite a bit older than him it is really just a bit of horsing around, a bit of harmless fun.

He walks over to me and I watch him closely.

He stands close enough to me that I can smell him. It is a mix of his cologne and muddy sweat. Wow its intoxicating in a nice way and I'm instantly weakened. He towers over me, places an arm each side of me and leans them on the washing machine behind me. His face gets closer to mine and I start to protest but he stops me with his finger to my lips. His hand then glides from my mouth to the back of my neck and his hand then cradles my head, his face gets closer and I realise he is going to kiss me...... My mind is racing. I can't do this; I'm too old for him. I know his Mum for goodness sake! But then his lips graze over mine and I instantly react in my loins.

I fall into his arms as he embraces me and deepens the kiss. I'm lost! I have nothing! I haven't been kissed in such a long time, it feels so good to be held and kissed like this.

His other hand starts to move and finds my breast. I let out a little sound. I haven't felt this for so long.

He liked how I reacted and his hand went under my top, under the cup of my bra and I shiver at the touch on my breast. My head falls back and he takes advantage of this and starts to kiss my neck. This can't be happening. I must be dreaming!

His hands are lifting my top now and I let him, I lift my arms above my head as he takes my top off and let it fall to the floor. His arms are quick to go around me to my back and he skilfully unclips my bra. My mind is fuzzy, what the hell is happening here? He continues to kiss my neck as my bra is removed and joins my top on the floor. He lifts his head and looks at my breasts, my heart is racing. He smiles and starts kissing them. It feels so good, I just let it happen! His hands are all over me.

Without warning he lifts me and sits me on top of the washing machine, pushes me back and lifts my loose fitting skirt.

I lean back and watch as he pulls my knickers to one side and touches the lips of my sex. I tense up and he looks me directly in the eyes and says softly "relax, I won't hurt you."

His fingers slide up and down my pussy and then he bends down and kisses my inner thigh. I feel him kissing my pussy lips, his fingers open my lips further then I feel the velvety warmth of his tongue. Mmmmm he's licking me! I lean back further to give him more access and his tongue dives in and out of my pleasure.

I feel his finger enter me and it takes my breath away. I arch my back to feel the intensity of his caressing finger, his other hand reaching up and firmly pinch my nipple. I can't help myself now and I moan…. I have to be dreaming! Right?

The vibration of the washing machine makes his finger inside me much more intensifying and I just can't control my moans now.

I grab the back of his head and push him further into my pleasure. He stops suddenly, picks me up like I weighed nothing. My legs were either side of his hips, I hold on to his shoulders looking into his eyes and he carries me to the showers. He gently puts me down, but my legs are so weak now that he has to hold me while removes the rest of my clothes and starts the shower going. He quickly takes off his own clothing; I can't help but look him all over. He is a gorgeous looking man! Very defined and muscly! My eyes find his cock and it's clear that he is enjoying what he is doing. He steps into the water and holds out his hands to me, inviting me into the shower with him.

I step closer and feel the warm water on my skin; he kisses me again with passion and my hands trace his chest and arms. I can't resist I have to feel his cock. While we are kissing I reach for his penis and wrap my fingers around it. Wow he is so hard right now. I stroke his hard cock as he looks at me with a devilishly smile and his fingers find my pussy again.

I'm wet! So very wet! I feel his fingers enter me again and I have to let go of his cock to grab his shoulders. His fingers slide in and out with ease and as my breathing deepens he realises I'm about to orgasm so he stops with the fingering.

He picks me up and I naturally wrap my legs around him and then he rests my back against the wall. The water from the shower hits his back and I can feel his cock just resting at the opening of my sex.

He looks me in the eyes and softly says "I'm going to fuck you now" he watches my face intently as he skilfully holds me with one arm and guides his penis to my sex with the other and then without hesitation gently pushes his hard cock into me...... I close my eyes and lean my head back so I can savour this feeling of being full. He thrusts deeper into me and then starts to pound me harder.

He continues to fuck me until I feel myself start to tense again, I'm about to cum. He pumps me harder and harder as I dig my fingernails into his shoulders. My body starts to shake and quiver as I am lost in my own pleasure.

I scream out "YES, YES!" This just seems to encourage him more and he fucks me harder still.

I hold on and continue to enjoy the ride. He leans into me, pushing me harder against the wall. He leans into my neck and starts kissing it again. I feel the warmth of his breath against my skin as his breathing becomes fast and rapid. His body becomes tense as his orgasm rides through my body.

He recovers from his delight, I kiss him and whisper "Thank you."

He kissed my forehead and says "I'm not finished with you yet!"

I'm still pushed up against the wall and held there by Bryan's body. The look he has in his eyes is so seductive and sensual and to be honest scares me a little, but in a good way. It's been so long since I've made love and he has taken control of my body and my mind is still fuzzy. I feel Bryans cock slide out of my now very tender pussy and I feel empty. He kisses me with so much passion again that it's easy to get lost in this sensation and I fall into his embrace. I let my feet fall to the floor so that I am standing again.

He reaches for the soap and turns me around so that my back is against his chest and stomach. He reaches his arms around my body and takes my breasts into his hands. The soap in his left hand and he starts to lather it up until its thick and bubbly and rubs it over my breasts. Wow, that feels amazing, the slippery feel of the soap and his big hands gently rub over my hard nipples. Back and forth, again and again until I feel myself becoming moist again. My head falls back and I lean into his chest as I absorb this wonderful feeling throughout my body. The water falls over our bodies as his hands leave my breasts to explore the rest of my body.

I stand there in a trance and enjoy the tingle his touch creates. He has very skilled hands. Down my tummy, to the sides of my body and find their way to my plump buttocks, I can't believe how good this feels. The soapy feel of his fingers find just about every part of my body. He edges closer and closer to my pussy and my breathing changes as his hand finds it. His fingers play with the lips for a few seconds and then slips two fingers in and out of my pussy quickly, but long enough to graze over my clit.

He does this a few more times before it stays in there and massages my already throbbing clit, I can feel his penis that is wedged between us growing again. I lather my own hands from the soap on my breasts and hear him moan as I do this… He approves! I rub my breasts again and he moans again but this time kissing my neck and whispers "you make me so hard woman!"

I reach behind me and find his hard cock between us. I grab hold with a firm grip but because my hand is covered with soap it's quite slippery. He feels so good. Still facing away from him I slide my hand along the full length of his cock while he enjoys my clit with one hand and my soapy breast with the other. Our breathing becomes heavy together and he quickly changes our position. He pushes me to the wall, this time face first and my hands instinctively go to the wall and I arch my back pushing my buttocks toward him to give him more access to me. This time he is much more forceful and grabs a fist full of hair and pulls my head back with aggression. It kind of makes me a little scared but I'm too turned on to voice this and he continues to manoeuvre to a better position. I feel his cock slide between my cheeks and I worry that he is going to put his huge cock in my ass. ….. I've never done that before so fear sets in. But he slides right past it and finds the warm, wet opening that's waiting to feel him again.

He pulls my hair a little harder just as he enters me from behind. I am feeling so many new emotions right now and it really surprises me. Bryan pounds me hard and it doesn't take long for me to climax again. I scream out loud "aaahhhhhhhh yeah fuck me harder Bryan, give it to me."

He thrusts deeper and harder into me, it hurts but it's a good hurt. His grip on my hair tightens and he releases his hot juices inside me again. He screams out between breathes "YEAH…. YES…. YESSSS"

He releases my hair and pulls me against his body as he comes down from his high. We stand in this embrace for a little while, the water still falling over us. After a little while he reaches to turn the water off. Turns me around, lifts my face to meet his gaze and I look deep into his eyes. He holds my face gently in his hands then kisses me so tenderly. In between kisses he very softly says "bet you never expected that" He reaches for a towel and places it around my shoulders and casually turns and walks away.

I watch him walk away completely naked. He grabs another towel and goes into the other room.

I just stand there cemented to the floor. I don't know how long I was there. I only realise when I was starting to feel cold. I finally come to my senses, pick up my clothes, then quickly dry off and get dressed and race into the other room. He was gone………

5

The Day We Met

It's been a few years of talking online, many conversations of soul searching and today is the day we finally meet. To say I am excited would be an understatement! I arrive at the airport early and check to see if the flight is on time. There are so many things running through my mind. Will he be as easy to talk to in person, as he is online? Will he like me? Will he like what he sees? My confidence isn't great but he always says nice things to me when we talk online. I'm so nervous and excited that time is just flying by and before I realise it, I see him……. My heart stops….. He hasn't seen me yet so I have a chance to really look at him. He's tall, very distinguished, his eyes are wise and knowledgeable, and wow he is attractive. My heart starts to beat again, faster than normal but its beating.

He is looking for me and just then our eyes meet for the first time.

Oh My!

His smile is breathtaking and he starts to head over to me. I watch his strong hand grab the handle of his suitcase and all I can think about is how that hand would feel against my skin. I blush as he approaches me. His smile is infectious and I can't stop myself. I walk towards him. I am so nervous. I look at him straight in the eyes and greet him with a confident "Welcome Master" In his country he is a dominant with his own sex dungeon and would appreciate this greeting.

In one quick motion his hand lets go of his bag and he is cradling the back of my head, his lips firmly planted on mine. His scent is intoxicating, his lips powerful and yet tender. The kiss is so passionate. I am lost to him already. I forget everything I was worried about and return his kiss.

I lay my hands on his chest, his heart is racing too. I feel his arm, he is strong! I'm enveloped in his embrace as we stand there surrounded by people but alone in the moment.

He lets go of me, looks into my eyes and in a very seductive voice says "Sandra, my pet! Finally I have you in my arms, take me home before I lose my self-control and ravish you right here where we stand."

The drive home seemed to take forever but we talked the whole way. His accent and the sound of his deep voice were almost tranquil. I could listen to him talk forever. We finally made it back to my place.

We take his luggage inside and I show him to the bedroom. I start to tell him where he can put his belongings but I am stopped mid-sentence with his finger over my lips.

"Sshhh" is the only sound I hear as his other hand reaches for my hand. He draws it closer to his mouth and kisses the back of my hand. "My dear, all this can wait, I must have you."

His hands then gently touch my face, as he looks into my eyes; he holds my head gently and draws me closer for a kiss. My tummy flips like I have butterflies in there. He starts to kiss my neck; Mmmm I tilt my head back slightly to give him better access. His hands move to feel me as he continues to kiss me he begins to remove my clothes. I want to return the gesture and try to undo his shirt. He stops. Looks at me and tells me "No my pet, Let me enjoy you first."

My words were stuck in my throat but I managed feeble reply "Yes Sir."

"Good girl" he whispers in my ear.

As he removes each piece of clothing he kisses and explores my body. I am totally naked!...... I stand there exposed! This is the moment I've been dreading. I don't have a great body and fear rejection all the time.

But he stands back and looks at me. ALL of me!

He then tells me to turn around. I obey, I must obey. He is my Master! I can feel his eyes burning my skin and I am worried he doesn't like what he sees. But I then feel him approach me; I feel his breath on my back.

He kisses the back of my neck and I feel his arms go around my body, he cups my breasts in his hands and whispers in my ear "Exquisite my dear."

I get Goosebumps all over, as he pinches my nipples between his fingers and continues to kiss the back of my neck. One hand stays on my breast; the other finds its way down between my legs. I gasp slightly as his finger slides in between the lips of my sex. "Mmmm you're already wet my pet, I like this! Now lay down on the bed."

I do as I am told. I lay there and watch as he undresses. His body is amazing and his cock is huge. I hope I can accommodate him. He climbs onto the bed next to me and props himself up on his elbow. He starts to trace my body, watching my reaction as he touches different places. In a low voice he says "this one is all about you. Our next one, you WILL obey me."

"Yes Sir" I reply in a tiny voice.

He kisses my breast, flicks my nipple with his tongue and I feel his fingers trace the lips of my sex. "I see you have prepared for me, Smooth and shaven, I like this. You will keep it this way, do you understand?"

"Yes Sir" I repeat again and just then he slips his finger into my sex, I'm so wet for him already that it slides in with ease. I feel his finger go deeper and he finds that tender spot straight away. I arch my back in reaction to this pleasure. He seems to like this too. He rubs the spot gently. I can feel myself tensing up. How does he do that? I wonder. I'm almost ready to explode when he withdraws his fingers and says "No, No my dear, not yet. I've only just begun."

He moves himself between my legs. His face is so close to my sex, I can feel him breathing. His lips kiss my sex gently. He reaches for my arms and pins them down beside my body. "Don't move!" he commanded.

He thrusts his tongue into my wet space and I hear him moan "Baby, you taste divine."

I try not to move. He lets go of my arms and uses his fingers to open my sex, his tongue finds my clit and I wriggle slightly. My Masters tongue works my pleasure and then I feel his finger enter me again. Oh that feels amazing but I dare not move. I don't want to disappoint him. I am almost at that point again and he stops.

Arghhh! I desperately need to climax. "I own your pleasure Pet, you cum when I allow it" he says with a cheeky grin.

He moves into position and I can feel his cock teasing the entrance of my wetness. He leans closer to me and kisses me with so much passion. I can taste myself on his lips. This makes me hungry for his kiss even more. Our kiss intensifies and I'm lost in it again. My hands are feeling the muscles along his back as his tongue pushes into my mouth in search of mine. Silky smooth, he is an amazing kisser. Just then I feel him enter me. He stops kissing me and looks at me; he goes deeper, still watching me. It's tight and stings a little but he feels amazing.

Slowly he starts to move in and out. My wetness covers his cock and he starts kissing me again as he thrusts deeper. I gasp at the size of him, goosebumps all over my body. He thrusts again and again each time a little deeper; Wow he is huge and feels amazing in my pussy. Thrusting powerfully I can feel myself build up once more. He stops kissing me and watches my face as I start to climax. I close my eyes but he says "No my love, eyes open! I want to see you when you climax."

I open my eyes and look at him deeply as he thrusts faster and harder.

I can feel myself reaching that point and he says "now you may cum! Cum for me my love."

Just as he says that I feel my body tense, I start to convulse in pure delight and scream out "YES! YES!" I grab the bedding with one hand and his back with the other. He tenses and I can feel him release inside me. He lets out a cry and begins to shudder also. He relaxes against me, we are both breathing heavy. He rolls off me and says "and that's just the beginning my love" I smile as he envelopes me in his embrace. So this is what happiness feels like!

6

Camping!

I had to get away. It has been a stressful week at work and I just needed some time alone. I knew a place that was secluded and perfect to pitch a tent and enjoy some quiet time. It was right along the river so it was then that I decided to pack my fishing rod and tent and get away for a few days.

It took me a little over an hour to get to this spot. But I knew it would be worth it. A friend had shown me this place last year and told me that very few people knew about it. Perfect.

As I pulled up to the camp site I noticed another car there, all set up with a tent. Bugger, someone else was here. I thought, Oh well it's big enough for us both and if I set up my camp site a little further downstream we would both have enough space not to bother each other.

I started to unpack my car and set up camp. Occasionally I would look over at my neighbour's campsite to see if I could catch a glimpse of who I would be sharing the area with. Nope. It seems deserted, so I kept setting up.

A little time goes by and I'm almost finished. The esky was full of bourbon and is calling my name. I finally set up my chair, grab a can of bourbon and sit down to relax. Ahhh! Perfect! Movement then caught my eye and I notice my camp neighbour coming out of their tent. It's a bloke! He sees me and lifts his arm and casually sends me a greeting wave. I send one in return, lift my drink as if to say cheers and took a big sip of my drink. This is my happy place.

It was getting late in the day. So I thought it best to start a fire to keep warm.

The nights get a bit chilly and there is nothing better than a camp fire and a few drinks.

It was around 9pm and I was really starting to relax, the bourbon had kicked in. This is exactly what I needed.

I went to grab some more wood from the box that I had brought, only to realize I had used it all already. Damn, I will have to get some more the next day, but my fire was starting to die down. I'm so annoyed right now.

Looking over at my neighbour's camp his fire was going nicely, it was then I wondered if he would mind giving me some of his wood. Oh well, this would be a good time to introduce myself. I thought.

I grab my torch and make my way over to his camp. Feeling really stupid, and like the stereotype "typical woman" I approached his camp and he finally saw me. He stood up and said 'Hi'. Straight away I noticed his eyes; even in the darkness with the fire as our only light I could see his face. He has kind eyes.

"Hi I'm Belle. Sorry to bother you. This is going to sound really cliché, but I've run out of wood!" I paused. Thinking about what I had just said. Damn that sounds wrong. "For my fire" I added. "May I have some of yours and I'll replace it tomorrow when I get some more for myself" I smiled, and felt really awkward.

He stepped forward held out his hand to shake mine. "It's great to meet you. I would love to help you out but I'm running low myself. I don't have enough to share but you're welcome to join me here and share my fire."

"Oh no, I wouldn't impose. It's all good, I'll just head to bed early tonight. Thanks though" I replied to him. He seemed like a really friendly guy.

"I insist" he said. "It's never any fun drinking alone, and I've got this bottle of tequila if you want to join me" he said with a smile.

I hesitated and then thought why not. I haven't had tequila in years.

Before I could even reply he grabbed the bottle and started to walk over to his table where I could see some lemon slices and a salt shaker. "By the way I'm Bobby, let me find you a glass and we'll do a shot."

I couldn't help but laugh, and follow him to the table. Thinking this is how people end up in the news, a strange man offers a lady a drink and then bam, There's the next news head line.

Oh well. You only live once and his fire was warm.

I accepted the glass he handed me. Then the lemon and salt and before I knew it we had downed the first drink, closely followed by another.

We sat by the fire and talked for hours. We actually got along really well and seemed to have similar stories. This relaxed me even more.

I stood up to excuse myself, a toilet break was needed but as I got up I stumbled slightly and he grabbed me to stop me from falling.

"I'm sorry," I said trying to focus on what I was doing, but the strength in his arms had my attention now. The alcohol had seemed to hit me suddenly and my ability to walk in a straight line became almost impossible.

He giggled and said "let me help you" he escorted me to the 'toilet' and then turned around to give me privacy. Wow, he's a gentleman too, I thought. We staggered back to his camp site and poured another drink. Although this time after we downed our drinks with the lemon and salt we both looked at each other and must have thought the same thing.

We both lent into each other and kissed.

It was electrifying. His lips on mine felt like they belonged there. It seemed so natural to be kissing this man that I had only just met.

When we separated he said "Wow, those lips. Those kisses! Incredible!"

I felt so relieved because it had been such a long time since I had kissed anyone that I was afraid I had forgotten how. But apparently I hadn't.

We kissed again, and again it was like we couldn't get enough of each other. With each kiss we become more frantic to explore each other. I felt his tongue in my mouth only slightly just teasing me. I was melting in his embrace. What was I doing? Am I crazy? But it was too good to stop.

I haven't had pash rash since I was a teenager. But when we finally parted my lips were raw from the stubble around his mouth. I thought wow that was incredible as we sat by the fire again but this time a lot closer to each other. We were almost cuddling.

Some time went by and I was almost dozing off. I said "I really should get back to my camp and get some sleep."

We both stood up but I was extremely intoxicated now. He held me up and tried to assist me walking but that wasn't working out well. He laughed and said "It's ok, you can sleep in my tent, there's plenty of room for us both."

I didn't even argue with him or insist on heading to my own tent. I just leant on him as he guided me to his tent.

Once inside he laid me down and asked if I was comfortable. I nodded. It was all I could manage. He lay next to me, facing me and it just seemed natural to kiss him again. He didn't stop me. I could feel his hand touch me. Slowly I could feel him touch my breast. My skin responded with goose bumps. A breath escaped my mouth. He looked into my eyes and his hand went under my top and to my back where I could feel him undo my bra. It all happened in slow motion in my mind as I wanted to treasure each moment but then suddenly I was naked, on his bed. He was kissing me and touching me. Then his fingers touched my pleasure spot.

He stopped kissing me and looked me in the eyes as if he wanted permission to continue. I closed my eyes and kissed him and I felt his fingers enter my wet spot. He groaned and whispered "oh my, you're so ready for me" and then he pushed his fingers deep inside me. It was a shock of pleasure. Deeper and deeper he thrust his fingers into me. Again and again until I could feel my muscles grip his fingers. He must have felt it too cause he stopped. He told me to turn over onto my stomach. I did as I was told. My mind was taken over by complete pleasure. He slid his fingers between my silky lips and teased the opening of my sex and then entered me with what seemed like quite a few fingers this time. It hurt a little but felt so good at the same time. I cried out with pleasure. My fingers gripped the pillow as I put my face into it to muffle my cries of ecstasy. The pleasure I was feeling right now was mind blowing.

He turned me over again so I was on my back. He was naked now too. I don't even know when that happened. He positions himself between my legs and looked straight into my eyes as he enters me. I gasped as his cock slowly slides in. The tip was smooth and covered in his moisture. He is so hard and fills my wet spot perfectly.

I feel his thick shaft glide deep inside me and he lets out a groan of delight.

I open my legs wider to give him more access. He grabbed my legs and lifted them up holding my ankles and thrusting his cock deeper into my hole. My mind is racing. I have never experienced pleasure like this before. He's pumping me and suddenly my body is thrust into waves of convulsive pleasure. I lose all control of my body's reaction and then I can feel him tense up. I watch his face and can feel his cock pulsating inside me. The grip he has on my ankles gets tighter as he explodes.

We both slump next to each other to recover. Nothing was said as he dragged a blanket over us and we both drift off to sleep.

I woke sometime later to find it was daylight. I have no idea what time it is. I look over and see Bobby still asleep. I quickly grab my clothes and quietly leave his tent. I almost run back to my camp, trying to cover my naked body as I go. Thank goodness no one else is here.

Inside my tent I find my phone and check the time. It was after 10am. I never sleep that late. Thinking about all that happened last night. What was I doing? I don't do those things. Maybe a swim in the river will clear my head. I put a long t-shirt on and find a towel in my bag, then head down to the water's edge.

It's a lovely sunny morning and the water is crystal clear.

Ahhh it's so refreshing. I swim out a few meters and just start floating around. Swimming back to where I started every so often, so I don't drift away. This is what I needed. I feel a little tender from having sex with that man. . . . Bobby! And the cool water is soothing the tender bits.

I give myself a little smile at my memory of last night. Just then I see something move at the edge of the water. It's him! Oh my! He looks even better in daylight. "Good morning" he said. "I woke up and you were gone."

"Yeah, I panicked, sorry" I replied watching him.

He didn't say anything for a while and just watched me, I didn't know what to say or do and then without any warning he started taking his clothes off.

"What are you doing?"

"I'm coming for a swim" he was looking right at me, as he removed the last item. His underwear!

"But you're naked. Bobby, you can't! Put your jocks back on" I said with panic in my voice.

He said nothing as he entered the water. I can see all of him perfectly and I feel my face flush with pink so I turn my head to give him privacy but I secretly wanted to look.

Still he said nothing as he waded into the water. He was heading straight for me.

"Wait what are you doing? You have no clothes on."

I know he is close, I can feel the water change. I can only just touch the bottom of the river and before I could stand up properly he was right beside me.

His hand touched my face and made me turn to look at him. He gently cupped my face in both his hands and bent down to gently graze his lips against mine. I felt that tingle again!

I stopped trying to stay afloat as I lost myself in his lips as it intensified. He slid his arm around my waist to support me and skilfully lifted my top right over my head. I was naked now too. Why has this man got so much control over me? His mouth left mine for split second. Long enough for me to realize what he had done. I look around to see if we were alone. "Don't worry Belle. We're alone" he said pulling me closer to him, slightly lifting me and he guided my legs to go around his waist. I had to put my arms around his neck just so I wouldn't fall backwards. But his arms were wrapped around me. I couldn't go anywhere even if I wanted to. He kissed me again. With each kiss, the passion intensifies and I can feel his cock getting harder. He pulls away to look at my breasts "damn girl look at those nipples, you have amazing breasts" I don't know what to say but as I'm thinking of a response I feel his arm move and then his finger starts to explore my sex. "Mmmm that's what I like to feel" as he slides a finger into my pussy. My head falls back slightly.

He leans in and I can feel his teeth on my neck. Little bites and kisses. I'm lost in my own pleasure as he quickly removes his finger and replaces it with his cock. The shock of feeling his shaft enter me brought me back to reality as I dug my nails into his shoulders. Oh! We were fucking in the water. He stood his ground with strength as he pounded me in my tender place. I could feel it deep inside. My body was giving into the pleasure as all my muscles tensed with my orgasm. He kept pumping and soon he was also deep in mind blowing orgasmic thrusting. He kissed me again and I realize we're moving. I put my legs down and they are like jelly. Bobby grabs me so I stay above the water. As we left the water I grabbed my towel and looked around for my t-shirt. It must have floated away while we were 'Busy'. I turn around to mention it to Bobby but he was already walking away, naked and carrying his clothes. I just stand there and watch his behind.

Back at my camp site I finally get dressed and make something to eat. I was starving. I hadn't seen Bobby since our water encounter, and wondered what he was doing.

A few hours went by and I still hadn't seen him. I had to go get some fire wood so I get into my car and drove to an area close by that had some fallen trees. I got my hand saw out the car and started to cut the branches. It was hard work. I stopped cutting when I heard another car approaching, it was Bobby.

He pulled up next to me and said "I thought you might like some help" he gets out his car and pulled out a chainsaw with a cheeky smile. I laughed "yes that will make it a lot easier!"

I stood back to watch him work for a few minutes. I barely knew this guy but I could watch him for hours. He went about cutting the thick branches with ease. As he cut, I loaded them into the back of my car. Job done! We both drive back and I stopped at his camp to share the wood.

I noticed the bottle of tequila on the table. There wasn't much left in the bottle. He saw what I was looking at and laughed "yep we destroyed that bottle last night. There's enough for one more, let's do another shot" he reaches for the bottle and starts to pour even before I answer.

This guy is so confident. I like that. I take the glass and downed it quickly, before he could say anything else I thanked him for the drink "I have to take the rest of the wood to my camp, thanks for your help and thank you for sharing your fire last night" I quickly broke eye contact and headed for my car. He stood there and watched me leave.

I kept myself busy the rest of the day, I went and found a rock to sit on by the water and fished for a few hours. It was lovely listening to the water and the birds in the trees. Peaceful! I even managed to catch a fish big enough to put on the fire for dinner.

Back at my camp I lit my fire and tried not to look over at Bobby's camp. I'm sitting back mesmerized by the fire drinking my bourbon and I hear footsteps. It's Bobby and he's holding something.

"Hey! Belle, Look what I found" he said holding it out for me to see, with a huge smile on his face. "It must have drifted away while I was fucking you."

I was so embarrassed I got up and quickly grabbed it. But before I could walk away he grabbed my arm, pulled me close and kissed me hard. Mumbling in between kisses "I can't get you out of my mind, your lips, and your kisses, the way you respond to my touch. You're driving me crazy woman!" I drop the t-shirt to the ground and my hands frame his face and I return his kisses. There's nothing I can say to that so I just enjoy the moment. His hand rubs my breast and I go weak at the knees, then they travel down my body and slide down inside my pants. His finger finds my wet spot and he groans "see you're ready for me again" he continues to kiss me as he fingers my wet pussy. I can't help but let out a cry; Then he groans again and kisses me harder my breathing is out of control, I can feel myself rupture with tingles. I grab his shoulder my nails digging in and start kissing his neck in between heavy breaths. I can't control it. I'm going to cum. I cry out louder as I orgasm on his fingers. He holds me tight as my legs give way. He sits me down so I can recover and I notice the huge bulge in his pants. My natural instinct is to reach out and touch it. He feels so hard. I pull his pants down just enough to expose his cock and balls. It's right there in front of my face. I hold it to guide it into my mouth. I can taste the saltiness of his pre cum.

He tastes so good; I lick the length of his shaft and put one of his testicles in my mouth. He likes that. So I do the other one.

I put his cock back in my mouth and he puts his hand on top of my head to "help" me out. He is fucking my mouth, I put him all the way in my mouth and I make a gagging sound as his cock is down my throat and I can't breathe. My eyes water and I pull back slightly to take a breath and go back for more. Suddenly he holds my head still and I can feel his warm cum spurting in my mouth. I swallow. It's salty. He looks at me wipes the tear from my face then bends so his face is right in front of mine and kisses me again. "Fuck that was hot" he mumbled into my mouth.

Well I can't believe we just did that. I go to the esky and grab a couple of bourbons and hand him one. "I think we both deserve this."

The next few hours we spent talking and drinking around my camp fire. We shared the fish that I had caught earlier and just enjoyed each other's company until it was well after midnight. I was tired and slightly tipsy. Bobby guided me to my tent, made sure I was in safely, kissed me and said good night. I was surprised and disappointed he didn't join me again but I was tired and soon drifted off to sleep.

The next morning I woke up late again. I could hear the birds chirping. It was nice to wake up in this peaceful place.

As I opened my tent I noticed a piece of paper stuck in the zip. It was a note from Bobby

Belle

You are exactly what I needed these past few days. You are an amazing and beautiful woman. I hope we cross paths again one day. X

I race out my tent and look over to where he camped. He's gone! Just like that! I don't know how to feel but then realize I had a relaxing few days with the best sex of my life. No strings, no commitment. It was just an amazing time. I touch my lips with my finger and smile as they feel slightly bruised from his kisses. I'm not complaining.

7

A Truckers Dream

I was headed interstate to visit a friend. I've been so lonely since she moved away. I had a few weeks of leave and I decided to hit the road to go see her.

I'm not overly confident in driving long distance but thought I would give it a go. I knew it would take all day to drive interstate so I left early the Friday morning.

I had been driving a few hours. It was relaxing. It was a beautifully sunny morning, but not hot. I had the windows down, the wind blowing through my long hair and my music was loud. It just felt good to be on the road.

I noticed a sign that said I was approaching a small town. So I thought a toilet stop and refuelling the car would be a good move.

Once I did those things I got back on the road. It was a long stretch of road in the country. Plenty of fields close by but no houses could be seen. It was just beautiful. Then my car started to make a noise. I turn the music down to listen and try to locate the noise. Then there was a bang from the front of the car and an even louder noise. Great! What's wrong now? I pull over to the side of the road, pop the bonnet and take a look. Who am

I kidding? I know nothing about cars. I look up and down the road. Not a car in sight. I don't even know who to call, or what to do. So I just sit in my car and think I just need a car to come by so I can ask for help. I waited for a couple of hours and there was no traffic at all, after the third hour I could finally see in the rear view mirror something coming toward me, it was a long way off but this was the first bit of traffic I had seen I really needed the driver to stop.

It was a truck. Truck drivers are friendly right? I thought to myself.

As the truck got closer I waved to the driver. Hoping they would see I was in need of some help. Luck! It was slowing down.

The truck stopped on the side of the road in front of my car, and I watched as the driver got out and walked towards me.

He was tall, dark hair, from what I could see from under his hat. He wore glasses and had a neat goatee type beard. He appeared rugged, strong, and looked like he could be older than me.

As he approached he smiled and said "have you got car troubles lovey?"

My reply was just a rambled mess.

"Well yes... My car started making this horrible noise and then there was a bigger noise, so I pulled over but I know nothing about cars, and I'm so glad you came along, I've been stranded here for ages, it probably wasn't even that long to be honest but it seems like a life time. I'm glad to see you. Thank you for stopping"

He smiled, let out a little laugh and said "I'll take a look."

He looked in the engine and then glanced at me. "Looks like it's a belt, you can't drive it. Sorry."

"You can catch a ride with me if you want. Not sure when the next car will come by or if they'll stop for you. I can take you to the next big town where you can organize a tow."

So disheartened but thankful for the lift, I thanked him. I grabbed a bag of my things and locked up my car, then followed him to his truck.

He guided me to the passenger side and helped me climb up. I've never been in a truck before so it was awkward getting up.

I have a loose fitting dress on which probably wasn't a smart move.

One of those dresses with a flowing skirt and loose off the shoulder neck lines. I tried to hold the skirt part between my knees as I climbed up the steps to the truck, so not to give my gentleman saviour an eye full but that wasn't working out.

I heard him make a chuff sound and realized my skirt blew up right over his head. Oh! I am so embarrassed, remembering the type of underwear I had chosen earlier that morning but he didn't say anything.

He just shut my door once I sat down and walked to the driver's side.

As he got in, I saw a huge smile on his face and knew he saw it all. My black lace "barley there" panties. . . Yeah! Another great idea! Well done Gabby, I thought to myself.

The driver started the truck, looked at me and said "strap in Darl, it's a long drive until the next big town. My name is Andrew, what shall I call you?"

"Oh I'm Gabby, thank you so much for stopping. I appreciate your help" I replied.

He gave me a wink and said "no worries Darl, I couldn't leave such a lovely thing stranded on the side of the road."

I smiled and settled back into the chair to get comfy. There was music playing and I relaxed quite quickly.

Conversation felt natural and we talked to each other with ease. After some time I felt tired and Andrew said "put your head back and grab some shut eye. You'll feel better."

Without too much hesitation I did exactly that, and drifted off to sleep.

Sometime later I stirred as I could feel the truck slowing down.

I was surprised that the sun was going down when I opened my eyes. It wasn't dark yet but I could tell it was getting late in the afternoon. It was then that I realized while I was asleep the neckline to my dress had slipped off my shoulder and my right breast was exposed.

Not all the way but enough that the top of my nipple was out. I quickly covered myself and looked over at Andrew. He had that cheeky smile on his face again. I could feel my cheeks being flushed with warmth as I again felt embarrassed. I quietly say. "I'm so sorry. Clearly my choice of travelling attire wasn't the best decision I've made."

Andrew laughed and said "I am not complaining. It's the best view I've had in such a long time. Don't be embarrassed you have beautiful breasts."

I turn my head to look out the window and ask "why are you slowing down?"

"I had to divert to this small town to fill up, we'll stop here for the night and tomorrow I'll take you to the town where you can organize your car and stuff" he replied.

Panic sets in and I sit forward and say "Oh no! that's not right, we should have been there already, I can't stay the night, where will I sleep? I'm meant to be somewhere else!"

"It couldn't be helped lovey! This is my route; you'll get to where you need to be, just not today. I wasn't going to leave you out there on the side of the road. It's much too dangerous. I'll buy you dinner at the truck stop and we'll crash here the night" he looked over his shoulder and pointed to the space behind the seats.

I pull the curtain back to find a bed back there. "If you think I'm spending the night with you in there, you are mistaken" I almost shout at him.

"No, no, don't stress. You're perfectly safe. You can have the bed I'll just sleep here in the seat out front. You'll have complete privacy. I promise."

He steers the truck into the waiting bay and we come to a stop.

"Time to stretch our legs Bub and I'll shout you some food. It'll be fine. Don't worry your pretty little head. You're totally safe with me" he gets out and walks around to my side of the truck and gestures me to do the same.

I open the door and he offers his hand to help me down. I don't have many options other than to trust this man. I follow him to the diner. He points to the female rest rooms and says "you can freshen up in there Bub."

When I come out of the restroom I scan the dining room until I find my mystery man sitting at a table with 2 plates of food. I walk over to him and he says "I wasn't sure what you'd like. I hope this is ok!"

I look at the plate and there's a steak sandwich with chips and a bowl of salad. It's then that I realize I missed lunch and I'm starving. I thank him and sit down to devour my food. It was so good. We talk casually and I'm surprised that I am actually enjoying his company.

He tells me to stay here that he has to pop down the road but he'll be back in 15 minutes. I must have had a panicked look on my face. "Don't worry gorgeous girl, I'm comin back for ya, just stay here and you'll be fine."

I spend the time he's gone messaging my friend to update her on what's happening and before I know it, he's back!

He's carrying a bag, he sat down again and we resume our conversation.

After a few hours I excuse myself to use the bathroom.

When I return he stands up and says "let's retire to the truck."

We get back to the truck and he shows me what's in the bag. "I hope you like Scotch, I can only have one because I'm technically still working, but I hope you will enjoy one with me!"

Andrew hands me a can of Scotch and Coke and we resume our conversation. "Cheers" we both say at the same time and take a sip.

The next few hours drift by and I am feeling the effects of the several cans of alcohol I had consumed. I am relaxed and sleepy. Tipsy is a great feeling.

"I think I need to sleep" I slightly slur my words and giggled.

Andrew pulls back the curtain, clearly not affected by his one drink and gestures toward the bed. I stumble my way back there and plonk myself down. He closes the curtain and says goodnight.

I don't have enough energy to undress so I just flick my shoes off and lay down. I can hear Andrew shuffling around and I'm curious as to what he's doing. Finally he's gone quiet and I lay there for a few minutes trying to listen but there's nothing. My curiosity gets the better of me. I try to be quiet and move the curtain back to see. Andrew has moved to the passenger seat and is covered with a blanket, leaning against the window. It doesn't look very comfortable. I move so I can study his face a lot closer. His eyes are closed and he's breathing out of his mouth. His lips are slightly parted and I watch him closely as he breathes. He looks so peaceful.

The longer I watch him the more I realise how lonely I've been and I begin to feel something inside me twitch. I have this over powering urge to kiss those parted lips. He's asleep so if I just gently kiss him, I'll get away with it. I thought.

I move slowly toward him. Lean in and softly plant my lips on his.

As I move away his eyes open. We are locked in each other's gaze. I lean in again and plant another one, this time he responds. Our lips move in sync. His arms move and extend from the blanket that was covering him and he traces one finger along my jaw line. The kiss intensifies and his blanket completely drops to his lap. Both his arms are exposed and I can see that he's topless. My hand moves to his chest to feel the mat of curly hair, my fingers find a nipple and as I gently graze over it Andrew takes a breath in. His hands move to my waist and he draws me closer to him. I lift a leg over his lap and sit down on him. The blanket is between us but I am so close to him now, our faces almost touch. He looks into my eyes, his hands frame my face and he draws me in for another kiss. His lips are warm and soft. He's gently kissing me and I lose myself and enjoy the kiss. As it intensifies I can feel him getting hard from beneath the blanket. It's a natural reaction to such passion. I instinctively start to rock my pelvis back and forth, grinding into his crotch. He likes this, his fingers move to my hair and he pulls a little. A sound escapes from my mouth and he pulls a little harder so my head falls back and my neck is exposed. He bites my neck. Small bites mixed with kisses, another sound escapes from my mouth and the neckline to my dress falls past my shoulder. Andrew takes advantage of this and kisses my shoulder. I'm still rocking on his lap, my head pulled back slightly, my shoulder and top of my breast is exposed. His grip on my hair releases and his fingers trace my shoulder line to my breast. He's watching my face as he does this. I can feel his finger tug at my dress and as it slips over my hard nipple; his hand then cups my breast. His thumb grazes my nipple and I shudder in response. I can feel the inside of me start to throb.

My nipples are erect in response to his touch both breasts are exposed now. I lean back slightly so he has better access. His face moves to my breasts and he places a kiss right between them, his hands push my breasts together so his face is sandwiched between them. His mouth is warm as he starts to explore with his tongue.

The warmth of his mouth on my nipple sends goose bumps over my entire body. He gently bites it and works the other one between his thumb and finger. My whole body reacts with tingles. I have to have his mouth. I grab his face and kiss him so aggressively. Mmmm he likes this. He shifts his weight trying to move the blanket between us. The blanket falls to the floor of the truck and I realize he's naked. He must sleep nude! I can't see too well cause it's dark. The only light we have is the light from the moon. I want to feel him. My hand goes straight to his cock. He's so hard. . . . And thick. . . . Our kissing resumes and I am moving my hand along the length of his cock. The wetness from my pussy is now starting to show through my barely there lace panties. I move my hand and start to grind against him again. I was kissing him so passionately. My arms around his neck, my lips and tongue explore his mouth and my panty covered pussy grinding his cock. His hand comes between us and with ease he slides my panties to the side and I can feel him guide his penis to the opening on my wet spot. We stop kissing, and we look at each other and he enters me slowly. I lower myself onto his thick cock. I can't help it, my body takes over. My back arches as I take the whole length of his cock, my nails dig into his shoulders and I let out a moan filled cry. Yes! I start to rock on his cock. I can feel him so deep inside me. His hands go to my waist to encourage the grinding. His mouth is biting, kissing, and sucking my nipples.

He suddenly lifts me with a swift motion and before I realize what's happening he's put me down on the bed. My panties are on the floor and he's almost ripping at my dress. That's on the floor now too. We're both naked. It's dark. I feel his touch. He opens my legs and then I feel the warmth of his tongue licking my delight. It's like it's the best thing he's ever tasted. His lips, his tongue and his teeth explore my velvety sex. It feels amazing and I start to breath heavy again. I push his face deep into my pussy and cry out as his tongue flicks over my clit like a pro.

He's done this before. He knows how to eat a woman. I feel a finger slide inside me, then two. He's pounding the inside of me while licking my clit.

I can feel my whole body tense and start to shudder. "I'm coming" I cry out. Grabbing his head I grind his face until my twitches have slowed.

Andrew looks at me, smiles and then leans forward. I feel his cock enter me again as he starts to pound me. My legs go around his waist to hold him in place. He's pumping slow, then fast then slowly again. He fucks me harder as I start to implode again around his cock and I scream out. He quickly removes his cock and I watch him as he releases his warm load on my stomach.

We're both exhausted. Andrew shifts me over a little, falls next to me then covers us with his blanket. He cuddles into me from behind so we are spooning and we both drift off to sleep.

The next morning I wake up to kisses on my back. I stir and turn to face him. I'm greeted with a passionate kiss and a hard-on against my leg.

Without any words we pick up where we left off last night. We have another mind blowing session of amazing sex. This guy rocks my world. We clean up. Have something to eat and get back on the road.

The conversation was easy and we eventually made it to the town where I could organize help for my car. Andrew made sure I had contact details of people that could help me.

We said our goodbyes and he handed me a piece of paper with his number on it. "I would love to explore this further, call me and let's work it out" he said. He leaned in, and gave me the biggest most passionate kiss and as we parted my legs felt weak. "Call me gorgeous girl" He climbed into the truck and drove off. I stood there feeling loved but lost. What an amazing time I thought. Now I must go sort out my car. . . . .

8

Forbidden Workshop

It was a beautiful day. The Sun is out. It's a perfect day to take the Lamborghini out for a drive. It was a purchase on a whim after the divorce, I wanted to treat myself to a luxury car and the sales guy talked me into this beauty. Very cliché but I love my red Lamborghini. Not something I could normally afford but the divorce settlement was a tidy sum.

I travel down to the coast; it's about a half hour drive from my house. I love having the windows wound down to feel the wind on my face. I have the radio playing and it's not long till I can see the ocean. This is my happy place. I pull into the car park and just sit watching the water rolling in and out for a while. It's so relaxing.

Time just flies by and I make the decision to head home.

Five minutes into the drive home the engine starts to makes a horrible noise. Not sure what it is I pull over. I don't know anything about cars so I make a call to get some road side assistance. It takes over 45 minutes for help to arrive.

The guy takes a look under the bonnet and tells me it's a blown water pump and that it'll need to be taken to the service department for repairs.

This couldn't be happening. I have a car I can't really afford and now I have to have it fixed. The road side guy organizes a tow truck for me and tells me to wait with the car. This is just great!!! It's not long before the tow truck arrives and I stand back to watch my beautiful car be put on the back of the truck. The driver offers me a ride in the truck to the repair shop. He's a friendly guy and we talk quite a bit on the journey.

He can see I'm devastated about my car and tries to cheer me up by saying "hopefully it can be fixed easily and you'll be back on the road in on time" I just shrug my shoulders because I knew the repairs were going to be costly.

We arrive at the work shop and I stand back to watch my car being taken off the truck. A man approaches me, he's quite tall, and he's wearing black pants, an off white shirt with a black tie with a swirly silver pattern on it. He looks quite distinguished with his silver hair and blue eyes!

He extends his hand and says in his deep voice "Hey there, I'm Brett. Is this your beast?"

I accept his hand shake and greeting and reply with a less enthusiastic "Yes it's my car, I'm Rebecca but everyone calls me Becca."

He smiles, he looks so charming and I can't help think of course he's happy, he's about to rob me blind with the cost of repairs. "Come with me Becca, we'll let the boys do their job and I'll grab your details so we can get this work started. Would you like a drink? A cup of tea! A cup of coffee! or a bottle of water?"

I reply with sarcasm "Do you have anything stronger, like whiskey?"

He laughs and says "sorry, can't help you there" he holds the door open for me and lets me walk through first. I have a feeling he's checking out my ass as I walk past. Brett guides me to his office and shuts the door.

"Please take a seat" he says as he points to the chairs in front of his desk. I was surprised at how comfortable they were. Of course they are everything here is expensive, the cars in the show room all cost $300,000 plus.

"Ok" says Brett "let's get down to it" he looks at me and continues "You have a blown water pump, you'll be looking at $7860 for Repairs."

I was floored "HOLY SHIT, are you for real?"

He just looked at me with a smug look and said "Welcome to the luxury car world baby."

I can't control my emotions. My head falls into my hands and the tears just start.

There was silence from Brett. I look at him "I don't have that kind of money, I really can't afford this car, who am I trying to be?"

Brett stands up comes towards me and rests his backside on the desk just in front of me. He lifts my face so I'm looking up at him and he dabs at my tears with a tissue.

"Maybe we can work out some kind of payment plan Becca"

I start to say "but I really don't . . . ." he cuts me off and says "you can clean the workshop and offices for a few months. That should pay it off for you. How does that sound?" Without letting me reply he continues "we will be closing soon and you can start today!"

I just nod in agreement feeling gutted with the outcome.

He lets me sit in his office until the staff and mechanics leave.

He comes back with a trolley of cleaning products and shows me what I need to do. I get started and feel thankful that I can work off my debt.

An hour passes and I notice Brett is watching me.

"Time to go home Becca, can you come back tomorrow at closing time and I'll show you the workshop, do you need a lift home?"

I thank him and accept his lift home, we don't say much on the drive but I give him directions to my house and when we arrive I promised to return the next day.

The next afternoon I get into my other car, the one I can afford and drive to the dealership.

Brett is waiting for me with the trolley and shows me around the workshop and explains what I have to do. I get straight to work and I'm busy for quite some time. I see my beautiful car and start cleaning around it. Sweeping and picking things up from the floor. It's then I notice Brett watching me again. I keep cleaning and then suddenly I can feel him behind me. I am startled because he is so close. I turn around and in a low voice he says "I can think of a better way for you to pay off your debt" and he touches my face gently. I should stop him but I don't. It's been a year since the divorce and I was craving the attention from a man.

He continues to touch my face and then trace my shoulder. I close my eyes because it feels so nice. I feel his lips on mine and I return his kiss. I drop what I had in my hand and touch his arms, he is strong I can feel his strength in his arms. His lips are soft and he smells amazing of cologne. It's intoxicating.

He guides me backward until I'm stopped by my car. His kiss deepens and I'm lost. His hand moves to my breast. I don't stop him. He unbuttons my shirt and cups my breasts in his hands. He stops kissing me and looks at his hands. With brute force he turns me around so I'm facing my car, and he almost rips at my bra clasp and then my breasts are free but quickly covered by his hands. He's leaning against me pushing me into the car. I can feel his hard cock against me. His hands release my breast and one hand moves to my hair where he grabs it in his fist, his other hand goes to his pants and I can hear him unbuckle his belt and then his zip. His pants fall to the floor. He pulls my pants down quickly while he's still holding my hair. I can't move, I'm pinned to the car. He releases my hair and leans into me. I feel his lips on my back laying kisses as he guides his cock between my legs. I feel him gently ease into me. It stings a little but in a divine way. It's been a long time since I've had sex.

I open my legs to accept his length and I can feel him push inside me. He's huge. I gasp, but enjoy the sensation. He thrusts quickly and forcefully into me as his breathing changes I feel his shaft start to throb and I realise he was done. He pulls up his pants and dresses himself and then walks away.

I'm left there half undressed wondering what happened. I dress myself, pack up my things and leave without saying anything to Brett.

The next day, I arrive at closing time again as the other employees are leaving. I wait in my car for a few minutes and just watch them leave, thinking about what happened last night with Brett. I can't believe I let that happen but it was exciting and so hot. To be taken like that, to be controlled. I'm lost in my own thoughts when I realize Brett is standing at the door of the office waiting for me to see him. I snap out of my day dream and get out the car.

Brett holds the door open again for me and I'm sure he does it only to look at my ass.

I guess the figure hugging jeans I decided to wear were getting his approval. I chose to wear something a little more revealing. My top has a low neck line that shows plenty of cleavage and buttons that start at my breast and end just past my jeans. The top is tight on my body which accentuates the curves of my breasts. Not sure if there would be a repeat of last night's episode but wanting to be accessible if something did happen.

Brett leads me to the room of cleaning supplies and as we were walking he was quite chatty "I think today you can work on cleaning the offices if that's ok, I've given our regular cleaners the week off so you'd have something do."

Once in the room he pushes me up against the wall and kisses me with such force but I respond favourably. His hands are all over me, rubbing at my breasts and in between kisses he breathes the words "I am losing control with you, I find you so breathtaking and I just have to have you again."

He suddenly stops. "I'm sorry Becca, there is something about you that I am infatuated with, but I will respect you."

I drag the trolley out past him and give him my most seductive look "I'm not complaining! Am I?"

I walk past him and head to the offices to start cleaning.

Over the next hour I notice him watching me. I deliberately lean over and reach across the desk and look at him. He's still watching. So I bend over to empty the bin I take my eyes off him to watch what I was doing and then I hear him walking toward me. I'm still bent over when he comes up behind me and places both hands on my ass and starts moving them around to feel the curve of my back side, I try to straighten up but he pushes a hand to my back and says "stay there!"

I stay bent over and he moves closer to me so I can feel his hard cock against me, he holds me in place with a hand either side of my hips and starts to grind.

"Oh god" I say in my head this feels amazing. I straighten up and as I do I lean back into his chest. His hands move to my breasts and he starts to kiss my neck. My head falls back against him as I grab his hand that cups my breast. I turn to face him and kiss his neck. Little bites too. I start to undo his tie, the knot is tricky but I manage to slide it off and drape it around my neck. I start on his buttons as he leans his backside against the desk. He watches me intently as I open his shirt to reveal his chest and stomach. I push it off his shoulders and my hands move to his nipples.

They are small and erect so I kiss and bite them while I concentrate on undoing his belt and then unzip his pants. He moves slightly to allow his pants to fall to the floor. I pull at his underwear to reveal his cock. I stop biting his nipples and trail kisses down his stomach until I am face to face with his cock. I was right! He's huge and I kiss the tip of his cock and he let out a small moan. I start licking the tip and around the head until I can't tease anymore. I put my mouth over the end of it and gently start moving my head up and down over it. Brett leans back, with one hand supporting his weight on the desk and the other on the back of my head caressing my hair while I work my magic on his cock. He seems to like what I'm doing. I really start getting in to it when he suddenly pushes me away and covers himself. I was shocked "what have I done wrong?" I say to him. I hear him say awkwardly "Stacey, how long have you been standing there?" It's then that I realize we're not alone.

"Mr Johnson, I'm so sorry. I forgot my keys" Stacey walked into the office, approached the desk and picked up some keys. I looked at her and felt embarrassed. She returned my gaze and said "Do you need a hand with that?" He smiled at me. I smiled back and said "sure" Stacey put the keys down again and watched me as I started sucking Brett off again. She bent down and looked me in the eyes and said "Do you mind if I join in?"

Stacey's face was right next to mine as she opened her mouth to join in on pleasuring Brett. It was an incredible feeling. Lost in the moment Brett had 2 women on his cock sharing his shaft and balls. Brett had a hand on each of our heads as we continued to pleasure him. It was intense. Our mouths touched a few times so we started kissing each other. We stood in front of Brett kissing and groping at each other until we had removed our clothing.

Brett loved it. Watching us girls lust over each other. We were both naked in front of him; he had a hand on his cock massaging it while he watched us. He suddenly got up and moved us to the desk.

He pushed all the contents to the floor and started kissing Stacey and had one hand massaging my pussy. I was so wet. He pushed me on to the desk and laid me back while Stacey went to the other side of the desk and climbed up. I felt his mouth on my pussy, his warm tongue exploring my velvet lips. I watched as Stacey climbed the desk and straddled my face with her pussy. Natural instinct took over and I started to lick her out. She was wet and tasted sweet. I held her in place so I could taste her juices and find her clit with my tongue. I must have been doing it right because she whimpered a little and started grinding my face. I could feel Brett use his fingers to open me wider, and then his cock was inside me. He started with a small gentle motion and quickly found my nipples with his roaming hands. I couldn't see what was happening but I could hear everything. Brett was now leaning forward kissing Stacey while she rode my face and he didn't miss a beat with his thrusting. He continued to fuck me harder with every push of his pelvis he would go deeper inside me and I could soon feel myself getting closer to climax.

My body shook as I lost control with my orgasm so Stacey climbed off my face, turned around and climbed back on to me but this time kissing me. Her juices were all over my mouth and she was lapping it up. I could feel Brett pull out of me and heard him slide into Stacey.

Her face stopped moving on my lips as he entered her. The look on her face was pure pleasure. His thick long cock entering her pussy full tilt and she loved it. I kissed her neck as she enjoyed Brett sliding in and out of her. Stacey's breasts were there for the taking. Her nipples were hard and even though her breasts were smaller than my own they fitted in my hands perfectly. I grazed her nipples with my thumbs and gently twisted them, making her look at me and bite her lip. I kiss her mouth while continuing the grazing of her nipples. Her face changes and I realize she's about to cum. I watch her intently! Stacey's mouth opens, her eyes close and then she holds her breath as her orgasm takes over.

Her moaning is exciting to listen to and then I hear Brett cum too. He's pulled out of her and emptied his load on both of us.

The excitement dies down and we climb off the table. Find our clothing and get dressed. For 3 people that were really intimate just moments ago, we went to a serious mood cleaning up our mess. I giggled a little at seriousness of the mood especially when Stacey turns to face us as she leaves the room and says "Good night Mr Johnson, see you in the morning!"

Stacey leaves and Brett approaches me. He picks up the keys to my car, jiggles them in front of my face. He lowers his lips to mine and plants a passionate kiss before whispering "After that episode your repairs are paid for, but I really want to see you again."

"Well you know where I live but I'll be back tomorrow to pick up my car, I have my other one here tonight."

He moves his kiss to my neck he says "How about I follow you home in your Lambo and we can continue this conservation in your bed."

"Done deal" Is all I can mumble.

9

Santa's Naughty List

T'was the night before Christmas and all through the house, not a creature was stirring not even a mouse!

I giggle to myself as I finish putting the last of the ornaments on the Christmas tree. I place my family's gifts under the thick branches of my fake tree and continue to recite the poem from my childhood!

*All the stockings were hung by the chimney with care, in hopes that Saint Nicolas soon would be there! *

Ha-ha not that I have a chimney or a fireplace cause in Australia Christmas is always hot. But the old poem still made me feel all warm and fuzzy with Christmas spirit. My family were coming to my house for Christmas lunch the next day and I wanted everything to be perfect! I had presents for my nieces and nephews. Even though I had no children of my own or a partner I still loved the Christmas holiday with my family.

I looked up at my big grandfather clock by the door just as it began chiming. It was 11pm!

"Wow time flies" I say out loud to myself as I adjusted a few ornaments on the tree. I must head to bed soon; it's going to be a big day tomorrow.

Just then I see a reflection in one of the shiny baubles on eye tree, something was moving behind me. I turn to see a man standing there in my living room. I can't believe what I'm seeing.

This man was tall, had a big white beard, wearing a plush red suit, white gloves and he was carrying a big red sack. This can't be happening!

"Santa?" I question in a whisper not believing what I see!

He leans back slightly, places one hand on his belly, the other was holding the red sack and with a jolly "Ho, Ho, Ho Hello there Mary" he greets me.

This guy knows my name! My brain is working overtime right now. So many thoughts. . . . He's not real, I've had too much to drink, this can't be happening! The only thing that comes out of my mouth is "Who the hell are you?"

"Now, now Mary! Is that any way to speak? You know who I am! Your name is on my list!"

Magically a scroll appears and as he holds the top of it, the rest of it rolls out and falls to the floor. On top of this scroll I see the words in big bold letters NAUGHTY LIST!

Santa puts down the sack and pulled out some reading glasses from his pocket then puts them on so he can read the list.

"I've been watching you Mary and I've checked my list twice, looks like you've been a little bit naughty and a little bit nice" he says looking over the rim of his glasses at me. It was at this time I realize I'm only wearing thin little lacy baby doll lingerie that is quite revealing.

Standing there wearing something that barely covers my nipples I suddenly feel exposed and try to cover up. Did Santa's eye just twinkle?

"Oh oh oh don't be bashful Mary, I know your thoughts, and I know your dreams. If you want to be on my nice list, you'll have to suck my cock til it gleams" he bellows as he drops the list and starts to undo his big black belt.

My first thought was 'Ok! So now Santa is rhyming and I have to suck him off. I've got to be dreaming!' His belt drops to the floor.

He opens his plush red jacket and I can see his jolly round belly. He continues to undo his pants, I can't look away. Santa is in my house taking off his clothes.

"Now be a good girl and get on your knees" his pants fall to the floor and he's already hard. Oh my goodness, Santa has a huge cock. I can't believe my eyes.

He holds his cock up and points to his balls.

"Your job right now is to suck on these" the rhyme continued.

Who am I to argue with Santa? I get on my knees in front of him and start to lick his balls. He lets go of his penis and it sits on my forehead as I'm sucking Santa's balls. I reach to grab his cock and I can barely hold it. He's so thick! I lick the length of his massive shaft and gently kiss the tip. I swirl my tongue around the tip and slowly put him in my mouth. I open my mouth wider to accept his size, and try to get him as deep as I can down my throat. Santa's gloved hands go to either side of my head just over my ears and he gently makes fists with my hair.

"Now my good girl, let me set the pace, I'm going to pound you like this and fuck your face!"

I look up at Santa and try to watch him. But he's ramming his cock deeper in my mouth, my eyes start to water and I find it hard to breathe. He's got his Dick down my throat and holding me there.

He pulls back, looks down at me and smiles. "Well well well, there's my good girl, I'm going to fuck you so hard it'll make your toes curl!"

And with that he picks me up off the floor and turns me around with dominance and power. He bends me over the arm of the couch, pushes my lacy panties to the side and enters me from behind.

I can feel his huge cock slowly enter my pussy. It stings because he's so big but feels so good.

Santa reaches forward with one hand and finds my breasts while his other hand is gripping my side and he pulls me toward him. In and out. Slowly at first until my pussy juices cover his cock, which makes the thrusting easier. Then his rhythm increases to fast hard pounding. I can feel myself stretch to accommodate him and I start to tighten up.

"No no no, my sweet Mary. I'm not finished with you. You're not cumin until I taste and chew" and with that he pulls out from me and tells me to lie on the couch.

As I stand up and face the big man he holds my face with his soft white gloved hands and leans down to kiss me.

His beard is thick and fluffy but his lips find mine and I close my eyes to enjoy the moment. His tongue explores my mouth, gently teasing me. Santa has the softest lips and was giving me the most passionate kiss I've ever had.

His hands move to my body and grabs at the lacy garment to remove it over my head. As I lift my arms to assist with this task I touch his beard. It's so thick and perfectly manicured. I give it a little tug to see if it's real as my lingerie hits the floor Santa's eye has that twinkle again and he says in a low deep whisper "it is real my dear." This is truly happening! I'm about to eat you out, you are not imagining."

His hand goes around my waist and his head lowers again to kiss me. He draws me in close to him and I can feel his hard cock against my skin. He leads me to the couch and lets me sit down. I watch him as he gets to his knees, to remove my panties and his gloved hands then push my legs apart. He looks hungry; I can't help but giggle as the thought enters my head of Santa eating all the cookies that are normally left out for him.

Well I'm not exactly a cookie but he is about to eat!

He softly kisses the lips of my wet pussy. The hair from his beard caresses my thighs and tickles me tenderly. His tongue starts to explore and I can feel the warmth of it as it finds my clit. I can't help it, I open my legs wider and place my hands on his hat covered head and push his face deep into my pussy. I hear Santa moan as I start to ride his face. His beard and tongue work well together and I can feel myself tingle and tense as I start to climax. He quickly removes his gloves before his fingers enter me and this drives me wild. I grind his face harder and feel like I'm about to explode. Just then he quickly pulls his fingers out and stops.

All in one motion he's sitting on the couch and I've straddled him. My legs either side of his, we are face to face. My hands are on his broad shoulders, I start to trace a line down his plush red coat with white trim then push it open and find his nipples that are just hidden by the fabric of his coat. I gently give them a tweak before leaning down to bite them. One at a time. I lick around his nipple then place it between my teeth and gently bite.

Santa takes a swift intake of breath. . . He likes this. So I do the same to the other nipple while continuing to play with the other one with my fingers. I can feel the hardness of Santa's cock between my legs and then his hand pushes between us to guide his cock into my sweet warm, wet pussy.

Just before he enters me he grabs my long hair with his other hand and pulls back hard so I'm looking right at him.

Almost in a breathless moan Santa says "Now look at me Mary, I want to see the shock, the way your face reacts as you take my cock!"

I'm looking right into his eyes and I can feel the tip rest at the entrance of my sex. He watches my face as he slowly pushes into me. I close my eyes to enjoy the tightness that surrounds his girth. I'm very wet so he slides in with only a little force. Santa takes his guiding hand away from his cock as I lower myself on to him to take the full length. Slowly I rise and fall. My eyes are still closed and I shudder slightly as his cock touches my G spot. He pulls my hair back even further and kisses my exposed neck. His beard tickles me and I clench my legs and I grind into his penis. I can't help it. I let out a moan. He is encouraged by this and bites my neck hard. Goosebumps take over my skin as my grinding gets faster and more intense. Santa lets go of my hair and places both his hands at the curve of my back where the love handles are. He starts to assist me by lifting me and then pushing me down hard on his cock. It gets faster and faster and I can feel the tingles inside my sex start to envelope me. I'm close to cuming.

"Oh oh oh, there's my good girl, faster Mary I'm going to blow my twirl" Santa rhymed.

The rhythmic convulsions take over my whole body and I shudder with orgasmic pulses that grip his cock tight. Santa lets out a moan and I can feel his enormous cock unload inside me. I fall to his chest with exhaustion, and his arms envelope me.

All of a sudden I feel really sleepy. It's been a long time since I have had such an intense orgasm.

My face falls to Santa's shoulder and I relax in his embrace. I can feel him moving beneath me but I'm too sleepy to figure out what's happening. Santa lifts me and gently places me on the couch where I drift off to sleep. . . . .

I open my eyes. I'm on the couch! I look down at my body and I'm dressed in my lingerie. I sit up. Feeling very confused. It felt so real! Did it happen? Am I going nuts? I must have dreamt the whole thing last night, had too much to drink and fell asleep on the couch.

That was the only explanation. But I did feel a little tender down there!

I look at the clock and it's almost 7am

I have so much to do before my family arrives. I get up, walk past the tree and see a gift under the tree with my name on it.

"That's odd" I mumble to myself. But pick it up to read the tag.

It reads "Mary! You made the list. From Santa."

I take the wrapping off to find a plush red hat. It was Santa's hat! As I remove it from the wrapping I get the scent of something familiar. It smells like . . . . Sex!

I remember the details of my "dream" and quickly run to my room to look in the mirror. I have a bite mark on my neck!

It wasn't a dream. Santa is real!

10

Happy Thoughts!

I often spend a fair amount of my time day dreaming and thinking about a guy that I met a little while ago. I feel it really is a once in a life time encounter with him. You know the type of moments that make memories that will last a life time!

It started so innocently, we just seemed to click. We seem to have a lot in common. Then that first kiss!!!. . . . So many things racing through my mind but the one that stands out was "wow this guy really knows how to kiss" so much passion, desire and need. It was memorable to say the least. You can tell a lot about a person from the way they kiss and I guess from that moment I was hooked.

There is a knock on the door; it startled me out of my daydream.

I open the door and he's standing there! Oh! It's Steve! I thought, and instantly I get butterflies in my tummy.

His smile is all I need to make me forget to breathe. He steps inside and brief pleasantries are exchanged, his arms encase me as I close the door, his lips touch mine. My mind goes blank and I return his kiss. Nothing else matters right now. His lips are tender and wanting. My tongue slips past my lips and slowly the tip glides into his mouth so I can taste him. The kiss intensifies

I can feel myself becoming moist between my legs. As if reading my mind his hand starts to wander, brushing past my breast and finds his way down to the waist band of my pants. His hand skillfully makes its way past my clothing into my moist spot. His fingers slip inside me and he breathes the words into my mouth. "You're so wet for me, that's so hot" his fingers slide with ease over my clit and he gives it a little flick which makes me twitch slightly.

He smiles against my lips and pulls his fingers out and brings them to our mouths where he stops kissing me to lick them. I watch as his finger enters his mouth, he seems to get off on the way I taste.

His tongue circles the tip of his finger he moans slightly and I join him to taste my juices on them, his finger rests on my lip, I look at him as he gently pushes it into my mouth. I can taste myself! I can't explain the taste but he definitely enjoys watching me suck them. He kisses me again but this time with force and lust takes over. He guides me to the bed, still kissing me we quickly fumble with removing our clothes. We can't seem to get them off fast enough. He pushes me on to the bed, spread my legs and wastes no time. He dives in between my legs and kisses my sex. He skillfully spreads my lips, I'm then lost in the sensation of his warm tongue licking my juices. He can't get enough of me. I feel his tongue tease my swollen clit. His teeth occasionally brush against my sweet spot sending twitches throughout my body. The talents and desire of this man's tongue are mind blowing. I've never been devoured like this before; so the sensations are all new to me. It's like my pelvis has a mind of its own now and I start to grind my sex over his tongue. The warmth, the wetness, and the sounds he makes as he explores me are the most erotic sounds I've heard. I reach down to push his face deeper into my sex and I feel a finger slide into me, it takes my breath away slightly. He rests it there until I start to grind my pussy up and down on his mouth pushing his tongue harder on to my clit. His finger slides easily in and out of me, my wetness covering his face and fingers. He makes these little sounds of desire and pleasure as he continues to devour my dripping wet pussy. Steve's breathing increases and he quickly moves up to my face and kisses me so deeply. I can taste and smell myself on his lips and this makes me want him more. I return the kiss with animalistic lust; my legs are wide and inviting, as he rests his huge thick rock hard penis against my skin.

I can feel his hips start to grind against me. He takes his hand and guides his cock up and down my velvety wet place until he finds my entrance. . . He pauses. Looks at me and slowly pushes past the opening. I gasp at the size of him and savour the moment. That feeling as it stretches every part of me and makes my whole body react with numbing pleasure. He pushes further into me. The whole length of his cock is inside me and he lets out the most sexual sound I've ever heard. It was like heaven. Slowly he moved back and then forward again each time pushing further. I could feel him deep inside, much further than I've ever felt before and it makes me shudder!

He raises my hips slightly which repositions the angle of his cock and I can feel new sensations. All of a sudden my body starts to tingle as his cock rubs against what I assume would be my G spot. The fucking intensifies and I watch his face as he starts to climax. "Oh baby, you feel so good" he says looking at me. He then closes his eyes and almost holds his breath as he cums. He's so gorgeous! He collapsed next to me as we recover and get our breath back.

A few minutes pass and we both have our breath back now. As he lies there I casually reach for his penis and surprised to feel he's still so hard!

He laughs and says "I have this problem of not going down. I can keep going and going."

"That's not a problem" I reply as I move down towards his cock. Still holding it I lower my face and kiss it. He takes a quick breath in "he's sensitive though" He says.

I feather touch my lips to his cock and lick the tip again to make it moist. Slowly open my mouth wider to accept his girth and gently start to run my tongue around his penis.

I go lower and lower with each movement until I can feel him touching the back of my throat. I try to go lower but my eyes start to water and it's hard to breathe. "Mmmm good girl" He says as I come up for air! I giggle! I think I like being told I'm a good girl. His good; naughty girl.

"It's your turn, climb on" he says and like a good girl I do as I'm told.

I position myself over him and guide his cock to the entrance of my now dripping wet pussy. I slowly lower myself on to his cock and savour every inch as it enters me. Once I'm as low as I can go I squeeze my muscles inside and watch his face as I do this and the enjoyment I see is hypnotic! I start to grind my pelvis on his cock.

This position is mind blowing and I get faster and faster. I can feel myself become even wetter as I ride his beautiful cock. I lean back slightly and he reaches for my breasts! I am shocked but then instantly feel joy as I feel the sting of a slap to my nipple. Oh my! I don't stop riding him though; I keep going as he slaps my nipple again. I am frantic now as I ride his cock. "That's my girl. Mmmm" he whispers while watching me.

He leans forward to try and catch a slap reddened nipple in his mouth and is successful. He squeezes it between his teeth and this makes me go faster and harder until I climax, clenching my pelvis and gripping his penis tightly within me! I soon become exhausted and fall to his side to catch my breath.

A few minutes went by and Steve gets up to go to the bathroom. I guess it's time to tidy up!

I follow him and watch as he makes a towel damp to wash his face. He is a gorgeous man so I like to watch him and admire his sexy body. Broad shoulders, subtle lines on his arms that draw my attention to his muscles, smooth skin and his cock is right there. Just beautifully placed and surrounded by a neat mat of hair. I can't resist.

I walk up behind him, place my arms around his waist and snuggle into his back, giving him a gentle squeeze. My hands are feeling the muscles in his flat abdomen. He's so perfect. I move my hands lower as I lay gentle butterfly kisses on his back until I find what I'm searching for. His cock is smooth. I place it in my hand and start to massage him. Steve turns around to face me but I don't let go of his cock. He looks at me "if you keep doing that we're going to fuck again" he says with a smile.

I say nothing but keep massaging his penis. I can feel him getting hard again. I look up at him and smile sweetly "oops" I whisper! I felt quite amused at his response to my touch.

He lowered his head and kissed me so passionately. His hands are touching, feeling, rubbing over my whole body. They find my sweet spot again. "You're wet again! You are amazing." And with that he spins me around and tells me to kneel on the edge of the bed. I do as I'm told.

I climb on the bed, knees just on the edge, lean forward and arch my back down to give him better access. I feel him behind me, rubbing his hands all over my ass making my skin respond with tingles.

I feel his cock against me as he starts to rub my clit from behind with it. This feels incredible. My sex is swollen and ready for more action. Steve grabs his penis and guides it to my entrance and gently slides in. He grabs me either side of me and pulls me back on to his cock. My mind is filled with nothing but pleasure. I lean back onto his cock and tighten my sex by squeezing my muscles. Steve thrusts his cock deeper into me and I can't help but grip the bedding. I moan a little louder than expected "mmm you like that baby" Steve says thrusting harder inside me. "Yes Sir, I do" I managed to breathe the words in reply.

Without notice I feel this sharp sting on my backside. Oh my; he spanked me! I should be horrified by this but I grip the bedding tighter and an almost groaning "YES, YES" comes from my mouth.

He smacks me again and again in the same spot and I responded by putting my face into the bedding and making sounds even I haven't heard before. His hands leave my sides and I can feel him gather my long hair into his grip. He grabs a fist full and pulls back hard, while his other hand returns to my side and he starts to ram his cock in harder and harder. With every thrust and pull of my hair I can't help but moan and cry out; not with pain but with pure animalistic lust for this man. A few more slaps follow and I can feel myself start to clench inside! This is the best feeling. I grip the bedding tighter and push myself back on to him. This feels amazing, and my skin is covered with tiny bumps but then he pulls out and instructs me to lie on my back at the edge of the bed. He is still standing so I rest my feet on his shoulders. Steve is quick to slide back into me and starts to thrust again. It feels so good. He's hitting that spot inside me and I feel like I need to pee! He gets faster and grabs my ankles and pushes my legs apart as he leans towards me. I start to feel my body clench again and my legs start to twitch. I can feel my orgasm building. I grab my breasts and give them a rough squeeze pulling at both my nipples as I release them. Steve seems to loves this sight and pumps harder. My mind goes blank! My body starts to shudder in a convulsive state! My muscles inside me tighten around his cock and I have no control over the next few seconds.

Steve finishes with a few muffled moans of delight as I try to regain my breath. He climbs on the bed next to me and I wriggle up until we are face to face. He puts his arm around me and kisses me on the lips, all around my face and then the forehead. "You are exceptional and sexy as! I can't believe I found you!" I kiss him in return and snuggle into him. No more words are needed and we settle into the embrace and relax in each other's arms..

11

Roadside Damsel!

After a long and cold winter the sun was finally out. The nights were still cool but the days are starting to warm up. Winter was coming to an end and spring is only a few days away. I really need to get out this house and back in the sun. My thoughts trail off to a memory from many years ago of a place that my Dad had taken me fishing once. I couldn't quite recall where exactly it was but I had this sudden urge to grab my rod and go exploring. I organised a few things, a bite to eat, a drink, bait and my fishing gear and packed up the car.

Happy to get out of the house I started on my journey, heading in the direction that I think is the right way. I had the windows in my car wound down, sun roof open and some upbeat music playing on the radio. Some time went by, not sure how long but I really should concentrate now cause the roads were becoming unfamiliar. I'm trying to read the signs as I zip past them on the highway. Nothing seems familiar. I guess I'll just take pot luck I think to myself. I was approaching a sign that said

'Mangrove Park! Next turn left'

That'll do! Mangroves have water, that's all I need.

I make the turn into the next road I come across and follow it for quite a while. There are no other signs so I just keep going. After a few minutes the sealed part of the road ends but continues with dirt and gravel. I must be going in the right direction because I can see little creeks of water next to this road. As I drive further down the gravel road the creeks become wider and deeper. I can only see a glimpse of water every 100m or so now because either side of the road had thick trees and shrubs.

I eventually come to the end of the road and it opens up into a stunning area of water surrounded by trees and rocks. This place is gorgeous.

I get out the car, stretch my legs and set up my fishing gear. The next few hours were glorious. There's no one here, it's so peaceful sitting in the sunshine, watching the water lap against the rocks by the edge. The birdlife, bee's in the bushes and butterflies resting on the flowers. It is simply magical. It really didn't matter that I didn't catch anything. I saw lots of baby fish in the shallows and the serenity of this place is intoxicating.

But alas I should be getting back, and so I pack up my belongings and head back to the car. ......

"Well that's just great" I say out loud to absolutely no one. I must have driven over something sharp on the way in. I have a flat tyre! ☹ Good thing I know how to change it but what a hassle. I put all my fishing gear in the back of my 4WD and go to the spot where I keep my jack......... it's not there!!!! "Well that's just great" I then practically pull my car to pieces in hopes to find it, but nothing. So I dig through my bag to find my phone. I will have to call road side assistance and get them to come help me.

NO SERVICE!

Out of range! Just my luck!

Now panic sets in.......I can't use my phone, I can't change my tyre, there's been no one drive past while I've been here, it's too far to walk anywhere! My options have diminished. I climb into the driver's seat, wind down the windows put my head back and think. The sun is still shining and really warm......... I'm startled.... A voice.

There's a knocking sound. I must have fallen asleep. I open my eyes and there's a guy standing beside my car, knocking on the bonnet.

"Hey! Are you ok?" He looked concerned.

I must have looked terrified. He stepped back from the car and said "its ok, I'm security for the area, just doing the rounds before dark, are you ok Miss?"

Relief sets in, I'm saved I thought. "Thankfully you came along. I have a flat tyre and my phone is out of range. Do you have a jack I could borrow?" I said to him as I got out the car.

"Oh yeah no worries, I'll grab it out of my Ute, you're lucky I came along otherwise you'd have been here all night" he said over his shoulder as he walked over to his Ute. "What are you doing out this far with no jack? I'm Stanley by the way" he continued.

"A spontaneous fishing trip to get out the house, my jack is normally in my car, I have no idea where it is though. Thank you for stopping to help Stanley, I'm Felicity" I replied.

He was already walking back to my car with the jack in hand and as I reached out to take it he said "Allow me to help. We can't have a pretty little thing like you getting dirty" he gave me a wink.

Oh is he flirting with me? I thought to myself.

I step aside and let him pass to access my car. I stand back and watch him work. He was wearing a security uniform, dark pants and shirt and a belt with gadgets on it, as he bent over to place the jack under the car, I couldn't help but notice how nice and firm his backside was. Those pants just framed it. I was lost in thought, watching him work and then he stood up and faced me...... Damn it! Busted perving!

He smiled and brushed past me. "So Felicity, do you have a boyfriend?" He casually asked me as he manoeuvred around doing the tire.

"Umm no, it's just me and my dog." I replied.

He is quite an attractive man; I would guess he was older than me. He is very skilled with his hands and I find myself staring at him and imagining how it would feel having him touch me. I've obviously been in the sun too long. I am having irrational thoughts about a man I have just met. He stands up quickly and faces me. We are very close and he takes a step toward to me which closes the gap between us, so we are almost face to face. At this point I notice he's taller than me because I have to tilt my head up to meet his gaze. I just stare at him, unsure what to do next.

He gently places his hands either side of my face and whispers "I'm going to kiss you now" I have no words but my lips parted slightly as if to accept his proposal. Slowly he lowers his face to mine and his lips brush mine ever so gently. There's a tingle, his lips brush mine again this time a little harder but still gentle. I close my eyes and let him kiss me; my arms naturally go around him and rest on his lower back. His hands relax and one moves to the nape of my neck and cradles my head. Slowly, tenderly, passionately the kiss intensifies. His lips are warm and his tongue darts into my mouth occasionally in search of mine. It finds it and he makes a sound, "mmmm."

We stand there kissing passionately and as it becomes more intense my hands start to explore his body. Up and down his back, across his butt which is firm, I grab it and squeeze and he makes that sound again.... "mmmm."

His hands relax and start to explore me then make their way to my breast. I get tingles all over my body as his hand covers my breast and he starts to grab and rub gently. My body responds well to his touch and my nipples get harder and I can feel myself becoming moist between my legs. My hand makes its way to the front of his pants. "Holy moly" I say to myself, he's hard for me already and by what I'm feeling, he's got a nice package in his pants. I find that instinct takes over and I undo his pants and work my hand into his undies to feel his manhood. My skin touches his skin. I wrap my fingers around his shaft and give it a little squeeze. He stops kissing me as he takes a short inward breath. I watch his face as I start to move my hand on his cock. I need more access........ I pull has pants open more and pull his undies down a bit to expose his cock. I have to see it. I break the gaze and look down. Oh my!! He has a beautiful cock. I run my thumb gently over the tip and can feel moisture. I can't help myself I have to taste him. Without hesitation I kneel down in front of him and position myself, pulling his pants down some more to give me more access and then look up at him. He watches me as I take his cock in my hand and guide it to my mouth. I lick the tip and watch his reaction. He smiles and lifts his shirt slightly to give himself a better view. I flick the tip again with my tongue, and then lower my mouth on to his cock. Slowly I move up and down.

With each stroke of my mouth I get deeper and deeper until I can feel his cock in my throat. I'm greedy so I push further and hold it there. He grabs my head with both hands, clumps my hair into his fists and pushes it deeper until I can't breathe. I pull back abruptly, take a breath and go back for more. Up and down his shaft with my mouth and he starts to thrust his pelvis while cradling my head. "Good girl" he says.

Oh my! Hearing him say those words is like flicking a switch. I grab his shaft in one hand and remove his cock from my mouth and tap the tip several times on my tongue before I suck again. He pulls back and almost pulls me into a standing position. He kisses me with so much lust and starts to grab at my shirt, lifts it over my head and discards it in the open window of my car. He stares at my black lacy bra and instructs me to turn around. His skilled hands quickly unclips the lacy garment from my back and discards that also to my car. His arms engulf me as he plants kisses on my neck. His hands cover my breasts as he gently rubs, pinches and squeezes them. I lean back into him. My back against his chest, my head falls back and I look up at him, he kisses me while his hands are busy and it's my turn to let out a small moan.

I turn to face him again and we continue to kiss, this time his hand finds the waistband of my pants and he pushes past that and my knickers and slides his fingers over the lips and feels the dampness of my juices. He easily slides past the lips and magically straight to my clit. The tenderness of his touches makes me hold my breath as I can feel his fingers dancing in circles over and around my aroused clit.

"You're so wet" he whispers and then without warning slides a finger into my sex. I arch and lean forward to push his finger deeper. He withdraws slowly and then pushes it back in with slightly more force. I can't help but lift one leg off the ground which gives him more access. His kiss turns to heated passion and I hold on to him and ride the aggressive thrusts of his finger. My pelvis thrusts toward him with each rhythmic move, and I can feel myself beginning to clench up inside. Just like that he stops..... He removes his finger and playfully pushes me towards my car.

He opens the back door, of the driver's side and instructs me to climb in, and lie on my back. I do...... he fumbles with my clothing, shoes off, pants off, almost rips my knickers off. He opens my legs, and I feel his breath, then I am instantly lost in the sensation of his tongue gliding over my sensitive wet spot, his lips sucking simultaneously and with the combination of those two things make my body quivers uncontrollably. Then he inserts a finger again....... then another. This is tight but feels so good. I can feel myself grip his fingers again and this time there's no stopping. I reach down to his head and grab a fist full of his hair and push his face deeper into my pleasure spot. I arch my back, tighten my fist and call out "I'm cuming, I'm cuming" his tongue lashes my clit faster as I climax on his face. As I start to relax he pulls out and before I have a chance to react he is climbing into the back of the car on top of me.

He positions himself awkwardly and manoeuvres his penis into my still throbbing sex. The thickness of his cock makes my sex feel tight as it stretches to accommodate him. He slowly slides inside me and we both react to the sensation. He pulls back slightly and thrusts inside again; I twitch as I can feel his cock rub against my G spot. He gives a little chuckle as he does this again just to see me react... I've never felt this before with my previous lovers. He continues building up speed with his thrusts until I think I'm going to burst with another orgasm. My breathing becomes more intense and my fingers dig into his arms. I'm getting close. Just as I climax again his own breathing becomes heavy and his body ridged and we cum simultaneously. He falls to my chest with exhaustion. He's only there momentarily and is soon out of the car pulling up his pants and then holds his hand out to assist me out the car. He drops a kiss on my lips as I stand up and mumbles "You are incredible, I need to make love to you another time, where we can take our time and do it right."

I release myself from his embrace to find my clothes, I'm feeling rather exposed standing in front of him completely naked.

"I would like that" I replied while dressing myself.

The sun had started to set and it was getting difficult to see clearly but I was certain he was smiling.

We exchanged numbers and he promised to be in touch with me soon.

We kissed again as we parted and got into our cars. He waited for me to drive off first and waved as I left.

The drive home was quiet. My mind was racing with thoughts of what just happened. Exciting, thrilling and totally out of control..... But I loved it and can't wait to see him again.

12

Even Spaghetti is straight!

Do you know that feeling you get when someone looks at you in a certain way that makes you feel special? Yep! That's the look I was getting!

I have always been as hands on kind of Mum and I enjoyed being involved in the development of my kids. I liked helping out at their school. I stayed in their classrooms to help some of the other kids with their reading and I was a member of a parents and friends group too, for people who wanted to be involved in crafting for fundraising or just wanted to hang around for a chat and a cuppa.

I would spend most of the morning at the school a few days a week and when I was finished each time I would head over to the local coffee shop and spoil myself with a Cappuccino. The woman behind the counter that served me every time seemed lovely. She was very friendly towards me. She was tall, same colour hair as my own and dressed in casual jeans and a T-shirt. She was just a genuinely nice person and we always had a conversation each time I visited. Her name was Sophie.

This became a regular event for quite a few months until one day we bumped into each other at a party. One of the Mums at the school was a vocalist in a back-yard band that played cover songs and I was invited to her place to listen to their band play and have a few drinks. This sounded like a great idea so I went along.

Sophie was there! I went over to where she was sitting to say hello and I was invited to join her and her friends. Over the course of the evening we drank a heap and listened to the band play.

They were actually pretty good. When the night ended we exchanged phone numbers and promised to catch up again.

The following week when I visited her at the coffee shop she genuinely seemed happy to see me, we talked as usual but something seemed different.

There was a look she had given me, I wasn't sure what it meant but put it down to the fact that we have stepped up the friendship to a new level since we had partied together and exchanged numbers we were more than just shop owner and customer. We were friends!

Over time we became closer, we talked and texted all the time, we visited each other's homes and even our kids started hanging out together. I guess you could say we were 'best friends.'

We both opened up about our private lives and I soon discovered she liked women. That didn't bother me in the least. I have been married before and she knew my preferences. I had learnt that she was very much in the closet in regards to her sexuality and she was struggling with her family's acceptance of her. I spent many hours at her house talking to her about 'coming out' and giving her the support she needed to feel loved within herself. We had talked in great detail about past lovers and relationships and how she tried to be 'normal' by having a relationship with a man which resulted in her having children. She was a great mother and I really felt sad for this woman, she's had such hard time not feeling like she could be "herself" and to be perfectly honest I was a little fascinated by the whole thing. I guess you could say I was curious.

She was planning a night out with her friends at a nightclub in the city. A gay bar in fact! To celebrate her achievement in 'coming out' to her parents.

She was on an incredible natural high as her Mum seemed to understand and accepted her, so she wanted to party! I was invited.

I had never been to a night club before, oh except when I turned 18, the legal age to drink and enter nightclubs here in Australia. My friend and his mate took me into town to experience the clubbing scene.... I didn't really enjoy myself that night and just thought it wasn't my thing. It was quite boring and I didn't even get to dance!

But now I was being invited out with a bunch of women to party the night away. It sounded exciting.

The day had arrived of the big night out.

We had all gathered at Sophie's place for pre drinks. Apparently it's the done thing so you can continue the buzz when you get to the club. These ladies were so much fun and they had decided to pretend this was going to be a fake Hens night event. They had done this before and had great fun, so we all put our names in a hat and the one that had their name drawn would be the pretend bride to be. They had 'Bride to be' sashes and party attire too. They were very organised. Thankfully my name wasn't pulled. They had given the 'bride' a fake fiancé and a back story then she picked 3 others to be the 'bridesmaids'. Again I wasn't selected. Phew! Not sure I could pull that off, but it was going to be fun to watch the night unfold.

Spohie pulled me aside realising how nervous I was. She gave me a little pep talk and was giving me encouraging words about what to expect.

"The club will be full of people from widely different backgrounds, you'll see a lot of things tonight that you are not used to seeing, it is important to have an open mind and most importantly just have fun" she gave me that look again, smiled and hugged me.

The Taxi (van) had arrived. It was time to head into town!

She was right! I have never seen anything like it. There were gay men everywhere, kissing and cuddling! Women doing the same too! There were Drag Queens that were stunning in their big wigs, heavy perfectly applied makeup, gorgeous dresses and massively tall heeled shoes, and of course there were people like me, 'straight' but wanted a night of fun. It was fantastic, and clearly this was the place to go, to let your hair down and just have fun regardless of your preferences. The music was so loud and there were people already on the dance floor. It wasn't long before our little group hit the dance floor. The DJ played loud dance music, the buzz from the alcohol made me feel super relaxed and the crowd around me just loving life on the dance floor. This was amazing!

We were not the only 'Hens' party there too and I wondered if theirs was real or fake like ours.

The drinks were in abundance, the people were wonderfully friendly and I actually danced with strangers that just wanted to dance too. I was so relaxed and very tipsy by this stage. Sophie was hovering close by watching me interact with others. I smiled at her and waved. She waved back at me.

A woman approached me and asked me to dance. Absolutely! I love dancing. We couldn't really talk much because the music is so loud, but the woman I was dancing with leaned closer to me and said something that I couldn't hear. I pointed to me ear and mouthed the words "sorry I can't hear you."

She dragged me away from the dance floor to an area that was less deafening. She tried again.

"I think you are beautiful, can I kiss you?"

I was a little shocked. Was she hitting on me? I didn't know what to do.

"I'm sorry, but I'm straight" was the only thing I could think of.

"So is spaghetti until it gets wet!" she quickly replied with a wink.

Sophie was at my side then and said to the woman "back off, she's with me."

I was thankful Sophie had come to my rescue, I turned to thank her and she lowered her face to mine.

She was kissing me!

Her lips were so soft, her hands cradled my face and I guess I was lost in the moment because I relaxed and parted my lips to accept her tongue. We kissed for what seemed like minutes but in reality were more like seconds. Still holding my face she says "Are you ok?"

"Yes, I think that woman was hitting on me" I looked to see where the other woman was but she had disappeared.

"No, I mean are you ok with me doing this?" and she lowers her lips to mine again and gently kisses me. It felt wonderful. I had never been kissed like that before. It was gentle and so passionate. It actually made me tingle a little, deep within me. I haven't felt like that before. Ever!

Sophie took my hand and led me outside to an area that was a lot quieter. She sat me down on the edge of some bench seating and straddled the bench so she was looking directly into my eyes.

"I've wanted to do that for so long. How do you feel?"

"Well I'm drunk so I'm really not sure." I replied.

Just at that moment Sophie's other friends came over to us. They were all very drunk too. One of them didn't look too well and it was suggested that it was time to go home. We all agreed.

The taxi (van) ride back to Sophie's house was quiet, and gradually one by one our driver dropped them off at their own houses until there were three of us left. We all ended up at Sophie's house. The other woman went straight into Sophie's bedroom and crashed out on the bed. She passed out quickly. Sophie had made sure she was covered and had a bucket next to the bed just in case she needed to vomit.

I was sitting on the couch when she came back into the living room and sat next to me. "Are you ok?"

"Yes, I think so. I had no idea you were going to do that. You know that I am straight, right?"

She leaned in closer to me and tenderly brushed her lips to mine and whispered

"I know, …….. Why are you letting me do this then?" and she continued her exploration of my lips.

I didn't have any answers I just let her lips caress mine. There was an explosion of tingles on my lips as she traced them with her tongue.

I closed my eyes and savoured the moment. Kissing a woman is very different to kissing a man. She was tender in a different way, she was seductive and passionate. Her mouth left my lips and trailed down my neck where she laid soft kisses and bites. I relaxed some more and gave her more access to my neck.

I could feel her gently sucking but I didn't care. I was still reaping the benefits of all the alcohol I had consumed.

Instinctively I reached for her breast; her nipple was already protruding through her bra and top. I cupped it and grazed my thumb over the nipple and she inhaled sharply. She stopped biting and looked at me with mischief in her eyes. Then forcefully takes my mouth again and I lift her top up to gain better access to her breasts, and then her bra too. Her breasts fall free from their restraints and rest perfectly in my hands.

Even though I have done this to my own breasts, this was a new and overwhelming feeling. I liked it.

She knew this was new to me and a little out of my comfort zone, but like two virgin lovers she allows me to explore. Her breasts are warm and soft and her nipples are hard yet supple. I flicked one with my thumb and instantly it reacts to my touch. Her areola tightens and the nipple protrudes further like its searching for my touch.

We continued our little lovefest until she stops abruptly and sat down comfortably next to me, she pulls her undergarment and top back into position and I feel a little deflated. "Did I do something wrong?" I say.

"Let's just cool it for a bit" she put her arm around my shoulder and draws me closer. She kisses my forehead and we both sit there in silence for what seemed like hours.

I had calmed down now and feeling sleepy from all the adventures that had taken place these past few hours. The clock on the wall said it was approaching 5am. We had stayed up partying all night.

Time really does fly when you're having fun. I closed my eyes and relaxed in her embrace. Her hand moves to my chin and lifts my head so I am looking into her eyes. She kisses me tenderly; her lips part mine and I accept her tongue in my mouth.

It was an odd feeling when I felt her hand move to my chest. She brushes past my breast and lifts my top over my head. I don't stop her. I just watch her face. She smiles and shifts position so she can access my breasts better but then continues to move and somehow guides me at the same time to a laying positon on the couch.

She puts her weight on top of me and separates my legs with her own; her fingers laced with my fingers forced my hands above my head and she kisses me again. Her weight shifts to one side and with her other hand she grabs my breast and squeezes gently but then continues to move it to the back of me and skilfully undoes my bra. Again I don't stop her. Sophie unlaces her fingers from my hand and removes my bra quickly then throws it to the floor.

Goosebumps erupt all over my skin as the warmth of her mouth envelope my erect nipple. Watching her nuzzle on my breasts is the most erotic thing I have seen, she grabs the base of my breast and pushes as much of the nipple, areola and flesh into her mouth as she can and then flicks my nipple with her tongue as she sucks and pulls away. I've never felt anything like this in my life. I want to watch her but I close my eyes to savour each movement and enjoy how my body responds to her. Her weight shifts again and her hand is felt at the waistband of my jeans. 'Pop'…. The button is released. The zip is lowered. My eyes still closed. She wriggles my jeans down slightly.

"Mmmm red lace, you devil" she whispers and I can feel her breath below my stomach.

Sophie pushes the lacy fabric to one side and her finger touches the lips of my sex. I tense up. But I don't move.

She inhales "You smell amazing, I need to taste you."

She quickly removes my jeans and underwear and discards them to the floor also. I open my eyes and witness her undressing and I watch her beautiful breasts, so supple and round rest comfortably on her chest. Her sex is neatly manicured and suddenly I think 'oh my gosh, I'm completely bare down there, what must she be thinking?'

But then I was distracted as she positioned herself between my legs. My nerves kicked in and my tummy did summersaults inside. Sophie inhales again then the tip of her tongue flicks lightly over my outer lips and then she places a kiss on top of my love mound.

She looks up at me as if to gain approval to continue. I reach forward and run a finger tenderly over her face and that was all it took to give her the permission she needed.

Her next motion was the most insanely pleasurable feeling I have ever experienced. She laid her flat tongue low on the outer lips of my sex and slowly dragged her tongue in one long sensual stroke to the top of my mound, when she reached the top she pushed her tongue past my lips and dipped the tip into my sex where it ever so slightly grazed my clitoris.

All of my sensations explode at the same time. Goosebumps enveloped my entire body, I can feel them in my hair along my scalp, there's an ache inside my sex and my pelvic muscles started throbbing like I've never felt before and I could feel myself gush with my own juices.

Sophie kisses my inner thigh to let me regain my composure and then repeats the same motion, but this time her tongue flicks along my clitoris a little longer. She opens the lips of my sex with her fingers to expose all of me and she repeats the same action again on the inner parts pausing to allow her tongue to tease and taste my juices at the opening of my vagina. Her tongue felt warm sliding in briefly before targeting my now super sensitive clitoris.

She moans as she laps up my juices, her focus changes from tongue flicking to sucking and I run my fingers through her hair and push her face deeper into my sex, I grind my pelvis against her tongue and I push her head towards me. She moans again and slides a finger deep into my sex while she licks my clit. I instantly feel my muscles grip her finger while she strokes that spongy spot inside. Her finger pushes and pulls against my internal walls as she thrusts it in and out and then I begin my climax. My toes curl, and my legs stiffen, my skin tingles, my pulse quickens so much that I can feel the pulsing in my brain.

My body spasms uncontrollably but she doesn't stop, she continues her onslaught of lashings and my orgasms just rolls into another then another. Just when I think I've lost all control she withdraws her finger, stops the flicking and I am breathless. She moves up to my face and kisses me in between my heavy breaths. I kiss her in return and taste my own juices on her lips. It's the most intoxicating taste I've ever experienced. She lay next to me on the couch and rests her ear on my chest.

"Your heart is racing so fast" she smiles as if proud of her achievement.

I can't speak, I'm panting but no words come out. I am still reeling in the most amazing orgasm of my life. I struggle to lift my own arm to cuddle her, my eye lids are heavy and it's a struggle to try and open them.

"Rest now my love" Sophie whispers.

We are naked, in her living room, in each other's arms!

I don't fight it. I close my eyes and slumber takes over.

13

The Beach!

We don't get many chances to spend time together so when an opportunity arises we take advantage of it. I simply love spending time with him. This particular evening he picked me up in his beautiful old car. The sun had already set and as it was the beginning of winter it was a clear but cold evening so I brought my jacket with me. I also brought a blanket along; you never know when you may need one!

I got into his car and was greeted with a kiss! I always melt when he kisses me, his lips soft and warm and his masculine scent instantly makes me relax. There is something about this man that gives me the purest feeling of joy. I get excited and nervous each time I see him. I feel happy when I'm with him and still manage to get those feelings of butterflies in my tummy.

We cruise around in his car just talking and sharing stories. I could listen to his stories all night long. This would have to be one my favourite things to do with him. His car has those old style bench seats and it was nice to be able to sit close to him. Our fingers interlocked and our hands just rest on my leg. The moment was perfect. I had no idea where we were going and to be completely honest it really didn't matter. Just being with him was all I needed.

We'd been driving for almost an hour as we entered the driveway to a lookout point; there were other cars there too. Not the most secluded spot but the drive there was lovely. We found a vacant space and parked the car. The heating in the car made us forget just how cold it was outside and as we sat there kissing and cuddling the windows soon started to fog up.

We were interrupted by the sounds of cars coming and going and people talking. So, on a spontaneous thought he decides we should go for a walk.

Jackets on all rugged up we get out the car and walk hand in hand through the car park and up the hill slightly but were disappointed when a locked gate stopped our adventure to the lookout point.

It really didn't bother me as long as I was with him it was still perfect. Slowly we walked back to the car and then continued on with our journey.

Conversation was easy as we listened to the older music playing on the radio in the background. I had no idea where we were heading and it didn't matter but I soon became familiar with the roads we were on. These roads I have travelled many times on my own. We were heading towards the beach!

The beach is one of my favourite places to go. When I need to relax and rest my mind I sit on the beach and take in the sounds and smells. It makes my mind clear instantly. It is a beautiful place to be.

It was around 9.30pm when we pulled into the car park at the beach. We were the only ones there! We were finally alone!

He switches the engine off but leaves the music playing and without missing a second he leans over to me and says "now I have you all to myself" I giggle and lean into him and we kiss passionately.

It really is quite amazing and wonderful that something as simple as a kiss from him and my body reacts the way it does. The warmth of his lips, the seductive way he pushes his tongue past my lips so he can taste me and his arms pulling me closer to him empties my mind of every other thought I may have had and I get lost in this moment. The music playing in the background sets the mood as we kiss each other like Love struck teenagers.

The song changes to one I haven't heard in a long time and suddenly I start to giggle as I hear the lyrics.

"Got myself a cryin', talkin', sleepin', walkin', livin' doll" and in mid kiss I giggle and softly sing the next line into his kisses.

"Gonna do my best to please her just 'cause she's a livin' doll"

He giggles too and sings the next line of the song

"Got a roamin' eye and that is why she satisfies my soul"

Then together we both sing in time with the music "Got myself a cryin', sleepin', walkin', livin' doll"

We both start to laugh. He looks at me and his eyes twinkle then kisses me even more deeply. This is simply the best moment in time!

One arm is holding me and the other is now searching for the warm spot between my legs. I open them to give him access as he fumbles with my clothes until he finds his way to my now moist spot. His fingers slide into my velvety warmth and nestle gently on my clit. He starts to rub my engorged spot, his fingertips flicking which makes me twitch. I have to feel him.

My hands fumble with the button and zipper on his jeans. I'm almost frantic as his fingers continue to work their magic in the folds of my sex. The kiss is hot and heavy now as we both start to breathe a little heavier. Aaahhh at last I have made my way past his jeans and underwear I place my hand gently around his rock hard cock and start to massage him. The tip of his cock is already damp! I smile to myself because he seems to react the same way I do when we're together.

I'm wet, he's hard! Perfect combination! He pulls away from me, removes his hand from my pants, licks his fingers seductively and says "How about we get the blanket and head to the beach?"

A little disappointed we had stopped again but eager to be with him, I reply with "sounds good" we adjust our clothing, grab the blanket and jackets and walk hand in hand to the sand of the beach. It is pitch black so it takes a minute for our eyes to adjust to the dim light. The only light we have that guides us is that of the moon reflecting off the water. It was cool but I didn't really notice, I was just happy to be with him. We walk along the water's edge cuddling each other. Another moment etched in my mind forever. He stops and turns to me and lowers his head to mine and our lips touch.

His hand cradles one side of my face and I lean into him more as my arms circle around his waist and we continue to kiss.

I am again swept up into the moment kissing my man and listening to the sounds of the ocean lapping the sandy shoreline.

We stop to look out over the moonlit water; his arms wrapped around me and mine around him. This is truly a wonderful moment.

He kisses my forehead and takes the blanket from me. Opens it out and lays it on the sand then gestures for me to sit with him on it. He leans over me and the action pushes me back until I am lying flat on the blanket and then he starts kissing me again but this time we let the moment take us. His hand instinctively finds its way back to my wet spot again and I open to give him all the access he needs as I fumble with his jeans until I am holding his shaft again. He's so hard for me. His cock is like granite. He lets out a moan when my hand gently moves forward and back over the length of it, there's a wet spot on the tip of his penis so I glide over the tip with my thumb and he shudders.

He kisses me deeper and plunges 2 fingers into my hot pussy. I instantly feel full; it shocks me a little and I hold my breath to concentrate on the feeling. My head tilts back and I moan in pure delight, the muscles in my pussy start to pulse and tighten around his fingers. He bites my exposed neck and I almost climax right then.

My grip on his cock tightens and he bites my neck again.

He seems frantic as he gets to his knees suddenly while manoeuvring his jeans so his cock is exposed. "On your knees, I need to be inside you" he whispers, as we aren't sure if anyone else is on the beach too.

I try to position myself in front of him while pulling my pants and underwear down past my knees so he can enter me doggy style. As I get into position and lean forward so my elbows are resting on the blanket I can feel him guiding his cock to my dripping pussy. I feel the tip of his penis pause at my entrance and then I'm instantly full as he pushes his cock fully into me and then he pauses to relish in the moment of being held tight by my throbbing muscles. He positions himself better placing his hands firmly on my hips and starts to pump.

He pulls out slowly and rams in hard, repetitively. He's so deep inside me I grit my teeth to quietly moan with pleasure. I don't want to be too loud in case there are other people close by. He pushes my jacket forward so my ass is exposed and then follows that up with a crisp slap to my bare skin.

The sting and shock of the slap makes me cry out and tighten at the same time. He grabs hold of my hips again and thrusts harder and faster. I can hear his breathing become shallow as he gets closer to climax. He grabs my skin in a pinch like grip, my toes curl and my hands grab hold of the blanket. My muscles tighten around his penis as I start to unfold with my pulsing orgasm.

His orgasm rips through his body; I can feel the pulsing of his penis as he unloads into me. We both collapse to the blanket in a hot mess, breathing hard. We face each other and he kisses the tip of my nose.

"Watching your ass in the moonlight is something that will stay with me forever, you are truly wonderful."

His words are calming to me; I snuggle into him as he covers my exposed skin with my jacket. We stay like this for several minutes until the cool air starts to chill us.

"Let's get out of here" he said.

So we stand to re-dress and adjust our clothing. He shakes the blanket to rid it of sand and folds it neatly over his arm. His other arm protectively covers my shoulders. I look up to him and kiss him tenderly on the lips. We start walking back to the car. There was no need to talk we were both still relishing from the excitement of sharing a public moment. Once we made it back to his car we brushed off the sand from our clothing and shoes. He opened the passenger side door for me to take a seat. He is such a gentleman. I am really not used to being taken care of in this way. I could get used to it.

He walks around to the driver's seat of the car and sits next to me. I slide over to be closer to him and he places his hand on my leg, leans into me and kisses me again.

"Where to; My dear?" He questions me with a cheeky grin on his face.

"Take me home lover! I want to keep playing with you" I gently place my hand over his crotch and look at him directly in the eyes. He responds to my touch and says "off we go then."

The engine roared to life, and the music continued to play as he pointed the car in the direction of home. This man has my heart!

14

A Mothers Fantasy

I've been married for what seems like a life time and a mother of two.

My life either revolved around my husband or my kids. I didn't have many friends and rarely had social occasions. Routines were very much in place and even though I love being a mother I still feel like something was missing. I didn't have a job; it was my 'job' to be there for my kids.

So when my youngest one was finally off to school, I joined a gym to try and lose some of the weight I had gained over the years. I even started making new friends and while the kids were at school I started to enjoy life again. I was having coffee dates and shopping days with my new friends. Life was starting to feel more fulfilling again. But it just wasn't enough I still felt empty.

I would drive my kids to school each day, and this had its own problems. My kids were a few years apart in age and when the oldest one started High school, I had to make sure I was super organised and had them organised too. I would take the youngest one to school then continue on to the high school for the oldest one. I was lucky the high school was only a twenty minute drive from the Primary school.

The only logical route to the high school, which would get me there in time for the start of the school day, had a team of men working to repair the bitumen. The speed limit was changed to accommodate the large number of trucks and workers that were there doing their job. It looks like it was going to be a big task. I decided I would have to leave earlier from now on just so I wasn't going to be running late.

This continued for the next few weeks, apparently they were resurfacing the entire road. I didn't mind. I was enjoying the view. Men, in their late 20's to mid 30's are working up a sweat doing manual labour, and I was enjoying the attention as I drove past.

I had noticed I was getting a few nods from a couple of the guys and I guessed it was more of a 'Thank you' nod for slowing down and being cautious through the road worked area. I returned the same way after dropping them both off at school and I deliberately slowed down to make eye contact and wave.

Was this what I was lacking in my life? Attention?

I would go home after doing my motherly duties and attempt to do my daily jobs of cleaning and general household chores. My mind would wander to the thoughts of the road working men. I would start to fantasise about how incredibly sexy it would be to pick one up on my way home and bring him back to my place for some hot sex.

All of a sudden I feel tingles in my groin and begin to feel myself becoming moist down there. I make my way to my bedroom, undress and lay on the bed. Completely naked I gently graze my fingertips over my nipples. They respond quickly and become erect to my touch. I like the way it feels to touch myself and explore. Grabbing my breasts and squeezing them as I close my eyes to engulf my thoughts in the delightful touch. My mind quickly wanders to those men again as I trail my hand to my moist place. I slide a finger in and touch my clitoris; it's starting to swell in readiness for what is building.

I slide my finger past my clit and it glides over my inner labia. My finger is covered in my own juices so I glide in another finger and gently rub them up and down over my clitoris and labia until my fingers are drenched with wetness. I am so turned on right now that I have to taste myself. I bring my fingers to my mouth and slide my tongue lavishly over my fingertips.

I smell of sex as I taste my juices and this brings me to a new level of readiness. Time to step it up…. I need to cum.

I go in search of my vibrators, and once I find them I locate my favourite dildo and vibrating bullet. I slide the dildo into my sex to lube up the tip with my juices then gently slide it to the moist opening.

Slowly, so slowly I push it past the opening and push it in bit by bit until it is as deep as I need it to be….. That feeling is so gratifying.

I withdraw it just a little and push it back in further than it was before. Each time I do this I leave a higher tideline on the shaft of my dildo.

With my other hand I reach for the bullet and turn it on. I click through the settings to reach my favourite one. Then touch it to my clitoris. Instantly my clit responds to the buzzing of the device as I roll it all over and around the area. I can't help the involuntary movements my body is performing as my muscles start to tighten around the bulk inside of me. I concentrate the vibrating bullet directly to my clitoris now and I can feel my orgasm building. Then suddenly without any other warning my body stiffens, my mind goes blank and I start to erratically shudder from within. My legs shake, my arms weaken and I can't seem to hold the bullet any longer. It just falls from my fingers as my body shakes uncontrollably for a few seconds.

I lay there, recovering from my delight. I reach between my legs to remove the dildo. I let it fall to the bed so I can lay in the wake of my desires. It takes a few minutes for me to feel strong enough to move.

Once I recover, I dress and go back to my duties. Feeling a lot less stressed about life.

Is this what my life has become? Fantasizing about strange men and satisfying my needs with battery operated toys?

The next day I drove through the road works again and practically blushed as I drove by. As I return one of the guys actually waved at me…. I wasn't sure what to do so I smiled and waved back, thinking about the session I gave myself the day before.

My imagination wanders again as I think about randomly stopping to talk with the workers. I wonder what they would do if I approached them and offered one of them a few hours of pure pleasure.

I would like to take charge when I got him home. Undress him slowly.

I would be very nervous, of course. But to run my finger tip over a nipple as I unbuttoned his shirt makes me tingle thinking about it. I would watch his face as I did this to see his reaction.

Slowly I unbutton and push his shirt over his shoulders and let it fall to the floor. Then unbuckle his belt and loosen it, but not remove it completely. Open it just enough to access the button and zipper on his work pants. While looking him directly in the eyes I would push his pants past his hips and as they slide past his buttocks and down his legs I would lower myself to my knees and inhale his manly scent before opening my mouth to accept his already hard rod. My hands would rest on the cheeks of his buttocks which would balance me as I slide my mouth lower onto his cock.

He would tip his head back and close his eyes and enjoy the feeling of his cock being worked over by my mouth and tongue. His hand would then pause on the side of my face before trailing back to grab a fistful of hair, I moan on to his cock and take it deeper into my mouth.

He becomes forceful and lifts me up to my feet in one effortless motion and crushes my mouth with his own in a passionate kiss. Both his hands are now cradling my face as I feel his tongue push past my lips. I'm still fully clothed as he thrust me towards the bed and guides me down. He straddles me gently while lowering me all the way back until I am laying flat. He kisses my neck and tries to remove my top at the same time. He pushes it past my head and I lift my arms to allow the removal. I have on a pink lacy bra and he reaches behind me and skilfully unclips it. The fact that I'm lying on it doesn't disrupt his effort to remove it. Once my breasts are free he focuses his attention to my already erect nipples. Placing soft kisses around the nipple then positioning it between his teeth in a biting action while cupping the other one in his hand.

He releases the cupped breast and drags his hand down towards my sex. I tense up slightly as his hand trails down and finds its way under my skirt. He roughly pushes my underwear to the side and abruptly searches for my sex. I am already wet so his fingers glide straight over my clit and enter roughly into my opening I gasp and arch my back at the sensation of being filled so forcefully.

Once he had two fingers nestled deep inside me he slowed his forcefulness and started kissing my neck. I relaxed a bit and enjoyed the pleasure rising inside me.

He pulls his fingers out and starts fumbling with the rest of my clothing. We are both naked now and I am very aware of just how hard his penis is. He was quick to positon himself between my legs, he leans forward as I open for him and he kisses me as he guides his penis to my sex and pushes it in. I let out a moan, he holds his breathe and I lace my legs around his body to keep him in place. I want to savour this moment, but he is impatient and starts to thrust. It feels great to have a hard cock sliding skilfully in and out of me and before too long I feel tingles within me. I am about to cum.

I yell out "I'm Cumming."

He quickens his pace and my body tightens and I feel him empty his load. The pulsing of his orgasm is in sync with my own. He crushes me with his body weight as we both come down from the high, he rolls off me then looks at me and says "that was so fucking hot." It is then that I realise that I am sitting in my car in the driveway of my home, my hand is firmly between my legs and it dawns on me that I imagined the whole thing. I have just masturbated in my car, fantasizing about a strange man taking me with brute force……

I gather my senses turn the engine off and exit the car. Thank goodness I made it home.

These fantasies are epic!

15

Lunch Break!

We have been meeting for secluded rendezvous for a little while and even though they are always exciting and pleasurable, I wanted to spice things up a bit and surprise him. It was always at the same place; and nice secluded spot that is quite beautiful. It is a long dirt road with parking right at the end that overlooks an inlet. It's a beautiful place to be.

We don't meet often but when we do it is always memorable. Today I had a surprise for him. I made some easy access pants. I cut the seam out of the crotch of my pants just at the right point which would give him access. Normally our meetings consisted of kissing and cuddling which is always lovely but today I want to step things up to a new level.

I arrive at our normal meeting spot a little ahead of time. As I always do. It gives me a chance to calm my nerves and prepare. I get so excited when I know I am going to see him. It really is hard to contain my excitement sometimes, so I need to get there before him to calm myself. Just the anticipation makes me wet so I try to clean up a bit before he gets there.

I see his car in the distance coming towards me. I actually start to shake a little with excitement. I lean against the front of my car and wait for him. He pulls the car up in front of me and gets out.

The smile on his face tells me he is happy to see me. I can't believe I have this man in my life. He really is wonderful.

He closes the distance between us, scoops me into his embrace and lowers his lips to mine….All is right in the world at this moment.

He has the most amazing kissing skills that far outweigh my own and I melt into his embrace.

"Hey there" he says with a cheeky grin.

"Hi" I lay my head on his chest and just relish in his company.

We talk a little, with slight pausing to kiss or cuddle some more and eventually the mood changes and his hands start to explore me.

He finds his way to the waist band of my pants and continues past it. He looks at me when he realises that I am not wearing any underwear. Then he continues to my wet spot. His finger slips in between my lips and I smile a little while he's kissing me. It was at this point he stops, looks at me and quickly withdraw his hand.

"What have you done?" he sounded a little shocked.

"Surprise" I reply with a rather large smile, "Do you like?"

He lifts my top to explore my handy work and dives straight into my sex with his fingers from the outside of my pants instantly finding the hole I had created.

"Mmmm, I like this."

His fingers slide easily into my sex and he kisses me again with so much more urgency.

"You need to get in the back of your car and lay down so I can really get a good look at this" he ordered me, and I do as I am told.

I climb into the back seat and lay back. I barely get into position and I feel his mouth on my sex. Oh my!!!! That sensation is something that will stay with me forever. His tongue darts skilfully around my clitoris, up and down the folds lapping up all my juices. He moans his approval and inserts a finger.

Now I feel his finger massaging my internal walls and his tongue focusing on my clit.

He suddenly stops, he stands up and without notice he rips the hole that I had created wide open.

I scream…. "Oh my god what are you doing?" I kind of laugh but it was so animalistic that it actually turned me on even more.

"I have to have more access" he says and I feel the fabric tear even more as he makes the opening bigger again.

He opened the zipper of his pants, pulls out his rock hard cock and climbs into the car and manoeuvres himself awkwardly over my body and positions his cock at the entrance of my sex. He looks at me and pushes forward. I am so wet that he just slides in easily and instantly my muscles tighten around his girth. That stretching feeling of my skin hugging his penis consumes me. He savours that feeling too and closes his eyes to enjoy the moment.

It's like he is mesmerized and suddenly comes out of his trance. He repositions himself and starts to pump. The more he pumps; the deeper he goes, it feels wonderful. I tighten up and he quickly cums inside me. He climbs out of the car, stands back and looks at his handy work. The rip in my pants is huge and he giggles as he reaches for some tissues to clean up his seed as it drips from my sex. Once I am clean I climb out and instantly feel the breeze upon my now exposed crotch.

My pants are destroyed. Beyond repair! He seems quite amused by his efforts and kisses me to claim his reward. I taste myself on his lips and my pants exit my mind. He turns me around and sits on the edge of the seat where we had just made love and pulls me to him. I lower my face to his and kiss him passionately. I could kiss this man forever! The simple gesture of this kiss prepares me for round two. He realises this and slides his finger into the folds of my sex again and concentrates his efforts on my clit.

It's not long before my legs starts to buckle and twitch as I can feel my climax building. My breathing increases and the grip I have on his shoulder tightens. I deepen the kiss as I climax over his finger. I can barely keep standing as the twitches erupt throughout my body. He grabs hold of me so I don't fall and swiftly swaps positons with me so I am sitting down to recover. He seems to be pleased with the outcome.

He looks at his watch and realises he is late returning to work. His lunch break was only half an hour and we kind of lost track of time. He rushes back to his car to check his phone and realises he has missed a phone call. He races back to me. "I'm sorry to rush off gorgeous, but I need to get back to work."

"Its ok babe, you go. I need to clean up, and figure out what I'm going to do with these pants, I didn't bring any spare clothes with me" I replied with a giggle.

"Sorry, Not sorry" he says with a huge smile. Grabs me around the waist and kisses me. "You are so wonderful."

He turns to leave, gets in his car and drives away.

I'm left standing there wondering what to do with my pants.

A few minutes pass and I hear my phone go off to notify me that I have a text message.

I check it and smile instantly. It's him ☺

Thank you for my lunch

But you didn't get to eat!

Oh But I did☺

Better than nothing. A fishy lunch today ;)

Oohh not true, you taste divine!

Hehe don't guys normally say it's a fishy taste?

Hmmm, not sure about the quality of their lunch but my Kitty tastes wonderful.

Aww you're just too lovely. I smiled at "My Kitty."

She is all yours.

Loved the "Play pants too" that was so freaking hot!

Glad you approve x

He really makes my heart smile. I climb into my car, start the engine and slowly head home. I smile all the way home until I realise I have to get out of my car wearing ripped pants and no underwear. I hope the neighbours don't see me…. Oh well. I'm too happy to care.

16

Home Cooked Is Best

The kids were at school so my partner and I were having a home day. He was in his shed tinkering with his car and I was in the kitchen baking some treats for the kids. They usually came home from school hungry and I liked to make them their favourite biscuits and cakes to fill them up while we listen to them talk about their day at school, it was a part of the day that I really enjoyed. Their stories filled me with joy.

It must have been getting close to midday because Blake was heading towards the house. He must be hungry. I was standing at the kitchen sink looking out the window while washing the dishes I had made from all the baking. I watch him approach the house; he really is an attractive man, strong broad shoulders, and defined arms, brown hair cut short and neat. His eyes are also brown and usually have a mischievous twinkle. As he approaches the house he sees me watching him and gives me a cheeky wink. I instantly smile and think how lucky I am to have such a wonderful man.

"I can smell those biscuits from the shed so I have to come taste test them for you" he says as he enters the house and makes his way towards me.

He stands behind me, places his hands on my waist and kisses my cheek. "Mmmm or maybe it's you that smells so yummy" he says as he starts to kiss and bite my neck playfully and he inhales my scent. "Mmmm you do smell delicious" I giggle and lean back slightly and I rest my wet hands on the edge of the sink. Blake's hands move from my waist to my breasts and he cups them tenderly still kissing my neck. I try to turn around to face him but he stops me. "No! Stay there, I want to feel you, taste you" This loving gesture soon turns to pure passion as his hands manoeuvre under my clothing and hold me in place.

He places one arm under my shirt and skilfully beneath my bra holding a breast firmly pinning me to his body while his other hand has lifted my skirt and is now touching the delicate skin of my backside.

I can't help myself as I am instantly involved in the moment and I moan at the delightful sensations that are now enveloping me. Blake's breathing has become rapid while his hands and mouth continue to explore my skin. He hooks a finger into my panties and quickly moves them to one side and is satisfied when he finds my heat. He moans a little and whispers in my ear "I'm going to take you right here, right now" and just like that he is on his knees behind me and he pulls my skirt down over my buttocks and it piles on the floor around my feet. He quickly pulls my panties down too and pushes me forward so I'm slightly bending over the sink. I feel his hand between my legs as he parts them and slides a finger into my heat. "Mmmm you respond so well to my touch" his fingers slide in and out and are now covered in my juices. Without warning he spreads my cheeks and I feel a slick warm sensation. His tongue! My mind is consumed with utter delight as his tongue and fingers explore every fold of my sex. The sensation of this act soon has me going weak at my knees and I can no longer support myself.

Blake swiftly stands and turns me around and kisses my lips with so much passion. I respond quickly. I taste myself on his lips, his tongue teases me with my own musky scent and it turns me on even more. Blake rips open my shirt, I hear the fabric tearing slightly and buttons bouncing as they are pulled from the fabric and hit the floor in different directions. I don't care; I'm lost in the moment. My bra is the next thing to go and I am aware that I am now completely naked in my kitchen while he is fully clothed. I try to unbutton his jeans but he stops me.

"Not yet my sweetheart."

He kisses me again but this time gently. He pulls me close to him and starts walking me blindly away from the sink towards to dining table. He stops walking and kissing me when are close to the table. He pulls the chair away from the end of the table and positions me where the chair had been.

He holds my face between his hands and then lowers his face to mine. His lips graze mine. He does this a few times before he deepens the kiss and I'm lost again.

The heat from his fingers leaves a trail of tingles on my skin as he releases my face and finds my breasts. My nipples respond to his touch and become hard and erect quickly. His lips burn my skin as they too travel down my neck leaving trails of kisses until he finds my nipple with his teeth and takes a little nip at one. The pain of the bite shocks me but is quickly replaced with pleasure.

He gently pushes me back until I am lying flat on my dining table. He leans over me and places one hand on my breast and the other is now teasing my clit. Oh the pleasure I am feeling at this moment is intoxicating.

Slowly he slides one finger into my sex and he goes deep straight away, he knows exactly where my sensitive spot is and touches it gently. I arch my back and push my pelvis towards him so I can feel him as deep as possible. He withdraws his finger but replaces it with two, and with this action he goes to the sweet spot again and this time pushes the soft spongy spot a little firmer. Massaging this spot I feel my sex instantly tighten and start to tingle. The orgasm is building but not quite there yet, the build up to the event is the most erotic sensations I have ever felt in my life. It's so addictive.

Before I reach the peak of my enjoyment he removes his fingers and they go straight into his mouth. "Mmmmm tasty" he whispers.

Blake drags the chair back into position at the end of the table and sits down in front of me. He manoeuvres my legs so that they are resting on his shoulders, he places his hands either side of my buttocks and leans forward. I can feel his breath on the inside of my legs.

He licks his lips "Mmmm lunch time" he says in a devilish tone and places his tongue on the lips of my sex. It's warm, it's smooth, it's wet and as he licks in an upward motion it sends shivers through my entire body. He repeats this motion and few more times and without even touching my clit I can feel my sex tighten in preparation of the orgasm that is beginning to build again.

His tongue slips beneath the folds of my lips and ever so slightly brushes over my engorged clitoris. Instantly I shudder and let out a moan. I couldn't help it, it was louder than I expected and this just seemed to encourage him.

He moves his hands to my heat and spreads my lips with his skilful fingers to gain better access to my throbbing clit. His tongue flicks over the peas sized erogenous zone and my hips start to involuntarily mimic the movements of his tongue.

Then suddenly I feel his fingers enter me and my pelvic floor muscles instantly tighten around them. I reach for his head and grab fists full of his hair as I grind my sex into his face. He moans with his own delight and vigorously moves his fingers back and forth. I am lost; I have no control over how my body responds and as I start to orgasm Blake growls out muffled words of encouragement. "That's it baby cum for me, cum all over my face."

My body starts to shake and my muscles grip his fingers so tightly that he can no longer move them. I let go of his hair and try to grab the edges of the table for stability as my mind goes blank and my convulsions take over my entire body. As my orgasm subsides Blake is still flicking my clit. "Stop, stop, please I can't take any more!" I say with a giggle.

He reluctantly removes his fingers and stops licking. My legs go weak and relax on his shoulders. He helps me lower my legs safely to the floor and helps me sit up on the edge of the table. I wrap my arms around him and kiss him so passionately. All I taste is me!

He stands up and pulls me with him. "Time for dessert" he says as he leads me to the couch in the living room. He removes his clothes as we approach the couch and by the time we reach it he is naked too. He sits comfortably with his legs apart. I don't need any other guidance and I fall to my knees in front of him. His cock is hard as a rock and standing straight up. He watches me lower my face to his cock, I go to the underside of it where the shaft meets his testicles and I place my warm tongue in that crevice. He flinches at the sensation and I watch him intently as I lay little kisses along the length of the cock until I reach the tip.

There is a droplet of moisture sitting on top and I look him in the eyes as I seductively lick the moisture from the tip.

It's sweet to taste and I want more. He closes his eyes and rests his head back against the couch. This is my cue to lavish him with my attention.

I place my mouth over the tip of his penis and cover it with my saliva; I go lower with each motion until I feel his cock nudging the back of my throat. I gag a little but continue. As I pull my head back I gently run my teeth over the ridge at the top of his penis. Up and down I repeat teasing his shaft. Without hesitation I take him fully into my mouth as deep as I can and hold him there at the opening of my throat. His hands move to my head and pushes me down further. His cock slides past my tongue and enters deep into my throat. My breathing is obscured but I hold it there for as long as I can until I need to release him for air. My eyes have watered. He looks at me and smiles. "You look so beautiful right now."

I giggle at this statement because I must look terrible, eyes watering, makeup running, my mouth dripping with saliva, but he thinks I look beautiful. That's love......

I have to have him. I need to feel full. I get to my feet and straddle him while he remains seated. I guided his cock to the opening of my sex and lower myself on to him. My eyes are closed so I can savour that feeling. The stretch of my sex envelopes his cock and the feeling of fullness makes me feel complete once again. I have indulged long enough. I open my eyes to find him watching me with a smile. "You like that baby?" he says

"Oh my lordy, Yes" I whisper.

"Fuck me baby, Make me cum hard!" he commands.

"Yes Sir" I replied and get straight into action. I move my hips slightly and grind into him. I grab hold of the couch behind his shoulders and raise myself up the full length of his shaft until the tip is just resting at the edge of my sex. Then quickly lower myself again. I repeat this a few more times until I need to go faster.

Each time I lower myself, his penis rubs the engorged soft spot inside me and I automatically twitch.

I lean back slightly now and Blake cups my breasts and begins to suck and bite my nipples.

This just about sends me through the roof again. I grind his penis faster with each pump.

He moves his hands to my hips and begins to assist me with the grinding by gripping hold of my skin and pushing my hips forward and back as he thrusts into me. His breathing quickens as my muscles tighten around his hard cock. I lean forward as I start to climax and smother his face with my breasts and as I do this I feel his cock start to throb and his hot load empties into me. He calls out my name as he climaxes and we both shudder as we finish.

All hot and sweaty Blake suggests we shower before the kids arrive home.

An hour later we are all sitting around the dining room table eating the treats I had baked earlier and enjoying the stories that the kids are telling us. Blake looks at me, he holds out his hand as an invitation to put mine in his and he winks at me. Just a few hours earlier he was eating me on this table. Home cooked is always the best.

17

The Need to Re-Connect

It had been a few of months since we had connected. I mean really connected.

We had been in touch of course, text messages and phone calls but life had taken over and there was a noticeable void in my life. I couldn't concentrate, my thoughts were consumed with images of him, with memories of past treasured moments and even though I had tried I still had desires and needs that I just couldn't fulfil on my own. I was lost without him. I had the realisation that I need him in my life. I wanted to be with him, nurture him, hold and kiss him.

What I would give to be able to see him smile daily and be the reason he smiled. He makes me feel complete and I'm a better version of myself when I'm with him.

His world as he knew it had turned upside down and all I wanted to do was bring him joy. Tell him "it's going to be ok" and allow him to forget life if only for a moment. It was at this moment I knew what I wanted to do.

My imagination took over!

I will pre-arrange to meet him. His place! My requests were simple!

*Leave the door unlocked.

*Wait for me on your bed.

*Lay on your back....Naked.

*Only wearing a blindfold.

*Now wait for me!

The drive to his place usually only took around half an hour but today it seemed to take twice as long. My anticipation grew the closer I got to his house. I finally arrived. I pulled up into his driveway and got out my car. I adjusted my outfit, I was nervous. I've always feared rejection and I was out of my comfort zone but I was excited too.

I had put on a new collar. I knew he liked them and I really want to please him. I approached the door and slowly turned the handle. It was unlocked. Relief!

I tried to enter his house as quietly as I could. His room was close to the front door so if he was blindfold as requested, his sense of hearing would be heightened and his adrenalin should be pumping through him. His pulse would be thumping in his ears, straining to hear my movements.

I closed the door behind me and tiptoed to the doorway of his bedroom. There he was. Perfect! He was exactly as I asked. He was lying on his back. Naked, and wearing a blindfold over his eyes. I stood there admiring him. His body was perfect. His legs were slightly apart, his arms were casually by his sides but his fingertips were gripping the bedding. His head resting on the pillows, his eyes covered with a dark cloth. I could see his chest rising and falling with each breath. He was excited; I could clearly see just how excited he was. His gorgeous cock was rock hard and resting on his toned abdomen, slightly leaning to one side. This made me smile. His testicles were firm and had that puckered look about them. Yep he was excited.

I walked to the bed deliberately not saying anything. I wanted to tease him a little. I gently ran my fingertips along his leg, starting from his ankle slowly moving toward his knee. He twitched. It was like a feather touch and his skin instantly reacted with goose bumps. The hairs stood up as I slowly traced the length of his leg, as I moved past his knee he tensed slightly and gripped the bedding a little tighter. Careful not to touch his engorged penis I leaned over and traced the length of his other leg.

I need to adjust my stance so I kneel on the bed next to him.

My fingers now tracing his stomach and continue moving up I gently run a fingertip over his erect nipple, he inhaled a short breath and as he slowly exhaled I leaned forward and tenderly planted a light kiss on his lips. He lifted his head in search for another.

Slowly and tenderly I brushed my lips against his again and as our mouths moulded to each other's, his mouth opened slightly and I felt his tongue brush past my lips. I welcomed this and met his tongue with my own. I quickly pulled away being careful not to get lost in his reactions. I had a task in mind and didn't want to lose my train of thought.

I got off the bed and the tiny bell on my collar jingled and I froze to see his reaction. He seemed disappointed that I'd left his side. I watched him move his head as if to listen for my movements. I quickly undressed and positioned myself next to him again kneeling close to his body. I moved his arm so it was strategically placed between my knees and leaned forward to cover his face with gentle butterfly kisses. My lips reached his ear and I gently took his ear lobe between my teeth and nibbled as I exhaled. His skin reacted instantly but he didn't move. My tongue explored his ear and traced the outer part then I whispered "lift your hand up and feel me" he did as I requested and when his fingers found my moist spot I shuddered. His fingers slid over the folds of my sex and he groaned at this sensation, with his eyes still covered he has to now rely on his sense of touch. I was still trying to focus on his ear, I whispered again "go deep" and again he complied. Oh the feeling of instant pleasure as his fingers slipped inside my heat. I knew I had to stop him soon or I wouldn't last. I pulled away from him and to my disappointment I had to push his hand away too. He was keen but I had to stay focused. As I moved to a new position I pushed his legs apart further and situated myself between them, as I did that he raised his fingers to his mouth and sucked on them. I watched him as he pushed his tongue between his fingers lapping up my juices that were glistening in the light. This almost ended me as he moaned and relished in my taste. What a turn on watching him enjoy my most intimate juices over his fingers.

Still trying to stay focused I positioned myself so that my arms straddled him and my breasts comfortably rested either side of his massively engorged penis.

I leaned down to kiss the tip of his cock and tasted the saltiness of his pre cum. I smiled to myself because I knew this was a good sign that he was enjoying the attention. I laid small butterfly kisses the length of his penis then starting at the base just above his testicles where I placed my flat tongue and slowly licked all the way to the tip sucking the moisture from the end. He sharply intakes a breath and releases it with a moan. I lick my lips to moisten them and gently take the tip into my mouth and enclose my mouth around his girth. Gently and slowly I go lower, I rest slightly and then go lower again. I do this a few times until I can feel the tip of his penis nuzzling the back of my throat. I push my tongue out and try to go lower again. I feel both his hands sweep up my hair until he's gripping on to fists full of my hair and he raises his pelvis slightly at the same time he applies pressure to my head and his cock slides deeper down my throat. I need to breathe and I gag on his cock. Tears breach my eyes as he releases me and I come up for air. He is still wearing the blind fold so I continue with my assault of pleasure and rub my breasts up and down the length of his shaft, adding my saliva as I go for lubrication, my nipples tenderly grazing the skin of his pelvis which sends arousing tingles through my whole body. I shudder as pleasure envelopes me.

I have to have him. I lean over the side of the bed and grab a small package that I had brought with me. I quickly unwrap it. It's a vibrating cock ring. I stretch the ring part over his hard penis and press the button to turn it on. He tenses as the vibration pulses. He moans and wriggles a bit. "Stay still" I said to him as I manoeuvred my body over his pelvis. His huge cock was resting against my heat and I can feel the vibrations too. I have to have him inside me. So I move slightly up the length of his penis and then down again leaving my moisture as I move. I grab his cock and slip the tip to the opening of my heat and slowly lower myself on to him. Oh my! That first initial sensation of my skin stretching to accommodate his girth is the most wonderful feeling. He lets out a huff of air as I take the full length of penis. The vibration from the cock ring now firmly resting on my clit. I don't want to come just yet so I lean back and start pumping up and down his shaft. The bell on my collar is jingling now with my movements.

"Take your blind fold off" I almost moaned the words.

He reaches for the blindfold and removes it quickly, tosses it to the floor.

"Oh you magnificent woman, you are gorgeous, and that collar!" He says to me as he reaches forward and starts to rub his hands over my skin. A small smile and a giggle escapes my mouth, the words he's just said are like music to my ears and all my fears and insecurities disappear.

This man is just so wonderful, I am the happiest I've been right at this moment.

I lean forward while I'm still pumping his cock and the buzzing touches my clit again. I grind my pelvis into him as I plant a kiss to his lips. I can't get enough of him and deepen the kiss. He returns my kiss with so much passion that I can feel my body start to tense.

My orgasm is building and the grip my heat has on his penis tightens even more. His breathing gets heavier.

"Oh yes baby, I'm going to cum" he whispers into my mouth just as I begin my own convulsions. I lean all the way back, my hands on his chest, his hands grabbing my breasts and squeezing. We both climax together and I scream out "Yes, yes, yes baby Oh my god you feel amazing!"

My convulsions take over and I lose control as my muscles tighten around his penis. I can feel him pulsing inside me. I collapse to his chest both of us breathing heavy. With all my energy depleted I roll to his side and nestle within his arms. He holds me tight and plants a kiss on my forehead.

I reach for the cock ring, turn it off and remove it. Then discard it to the floor and snuggle into his embrace.

A few minutes pass and our breathing has returned to normal, I look up at him and he's watching me. His fingertips are tracing my body, leaving trails of tingles as he moves them over my skin. I lift my head to kiss him and he meets me with his lips slightly parted and we kiss. His lips are warm, his tongue velvety and soon our kiss turns into something deep and full of passion and desire. I could kiss this man for the rest of my life. His touch transports me to another place. A place that's safe and loving and full of desire.

My mind goes blank as I get lost deep in the passion. His fingers still tracing my skin and they find their way to my sex.

"Mmmm you're wet again, that's so hot baby."

I smile sweetly into his gaze as his fingers flick across that sweet spot which makes me twitch. He notices my reaction and concentrates more on that spot. I can feel myself start to tense up again. Suddenly he moves and gets off the bed. I'm alone! I feel a sharp slap on the fleshy part of my ass. Oooh the sting is so satisfying.

Then he commanded "get on your knees, on the edge of the bed. Let's see how strong that collar is."

I obey instantly. My sex twitches with excitement of what was going to happen. I put my knees on the edge of the bed and lean forward, gripping the bedding in anticipation of what's about to unfold.

I feel him position himself between my legs and then feel his shaft trace my moisture and then without warning he thrusts inside me. Oh the feeling of sudden fullness sends me into instant pleasure. I grip the bedding tighter and lean back into the thrusting. He grabs my hair and pulls my head back. Oh yes! He knows exactly what I like. A sharp sting falls across my buttocks again and my pelvic floor muscles tighten around him. He reaches forward and grabs the back of my collar and pulls me back with force.

One hand grabbing the collar at the back of my neck and the other grabs a handful of my skin near my hip to hold on and he starts thrusting me hard and fast. He goes deeper with each thrust and I scream out "YES, YES!" Tingles start to envelope me again and my mind goes blank with pleasure.

I can hear him moaning as he thrusts his hard cock deep inside me. His pace quickens. I can hear him almost hold his breathe as he gets closer to reaching his second explosion. He breathes out loudly and loud groans follow as he erupts inside me again.

I feel him shudder and shake as he pulls out of me a collapses on the bed next to me, his breathing heavy and rapid. I fall next to him and we both lay there to recover. He envelopes me in his embrace again, my head on his chest I can hear his heart thumping loudly. My arm drapes across his stomach and I close my eyes. Our breathing falls in sync with each other as we drift off to sleep. We have a connection like no other.

Thank You!

Thank You for reading my little collection of short stories.

This book would never have happened without the support, encouragement and advice from my close friends.

They believed in me more than I did myself!

I love them dearly and appreciate all their encouragement and support they have given me during this time.

Fiona